"Let me get this st... a wife and think I fit the bill?" Her laughter bordered on hysterical. "I can see why you might think that. After all, we've got so much in common."

He ignored her sarcasm and moved in for the kill, hitting her where she was most vulnerable.

"What about our attraction?" His low, husky voice rekindled the memory of his kisses, his hands and the desire that flowed between them, simmering beneath the surface. "Why not settle for respect, friendship and a sizzling sex life?"

Nicola Marsh says: "As a girl, I dreamed of being a journalist and traveling the world in search of the next big story. Luckily, I have had the opportunity to travel the world but my dream to write has never been far from my mind. When I met my own tall, dark and handsome hero and learned that romance is everything it's cracked up to be, I finally took the plunge and put pen to paper.

"I live in the south-eastern suburbs of Melbourne with my husband and baby. When I'm not writing, I work as a physiotherapist for a vocational rehabilitation company, helping people with disabilities return to the workforce. I also love sharing fine food and wine with friends and family, going to the movies and—my favourite—curling up in front of the fire with a good book."

The Wedding Contract is linked to
The Tycoon's Dating Deal (#3810)
which is available on www.eHarlequin.com

THE WEDDING CONTRACT

Nicola Marsh

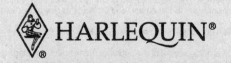

TORONTO • NEW YORK • LONDON
AMSTERDAM • PARIS • SYDNEY • HAMBURG
STOCKHOLM • ATHENS • TOKYO • MILAN • MADRID
PRAGUE • WARSAW • BUDAPEST • AUCKLAND

To Martin, for keeping the romance alive

ISBN 0-373-03818-6

THE WEDDING CONTRACT

First North American Publication 2004.

Copyright © 2004 by Nicola Marsh.

www.eHarlequin.com

Printed in U.S.A.

CHAPTER ONE

Steve Rockwell didn't have time for fun. Not unless it suited his purpose and didn't distract him from more important matters, like making money.

'Can I help you?' A hand touched his arm, halting him.

He frowned and stopped mid-stride. The sooner he completed today's business at the dingy Gold Coast theme park and flew back to Sydney, the better.

'No, I'm fine.' His impatience faded as his gaze met an inquisitive pair of hazel eyes, the likes of which he'd never seen before. They weren't green or brown but an incredible combination of the two, with gold flecks thrown in for good measure.

Not bad, if you liked that sort of thing. Personally, he had a penchant for blue where women were concerned.

He let his gaze slide down the rest of the woman, wondering if the loose, gypsy-like clothes hid any curves. Strange garb, but what did he expect at a carnival?

'You seem to be lost.' Her voice was soft, innocent and belied the age-old weariness he glimpsed in her peculiar eyes.

He stared at the hand resting on his sleeve, noting the short nails and callus on the third finger, the antithesis of the women who usually grabbed him with their perfectly manicured talons.

He stepped away, surprised to discover he missed her brief touch. The relentless Queensland heat, which he couldn't stand, must have melted his brain.

'I'm here to see Colin Lawrence. Isn't that his office over there?' He pointed to a small, ramshackle portable building on the outskirts of the grounds, past the whirling rides, the popcorn stand and the Ferris wheel.

She quirked an eyebrow at him. 'He's not in. Can I help instead?'

Despite her sass, he almost laughed aloud at the thought of doing business with this waif dressed in layers of flimsy, floating material.

'Not unless I need my palm read.' He noted the sudden defensive posture as she folded her arms. The action outlined her full breasts and he had a sudden desire to discover what other hidden delights lay beneath the layers.

Her eyes narrowed. 'Oh, I'm sure I'd have no trouble in telling you your fortune.'

So the lady liked to spar? He would have little trouble in accommodating her—after all, it was what he did best. He wasn't a partner in one of Sydney's most prestigious law firms for nothing.

'Go ahead, then, Madam Zelda. Give it your best

shot.' He thrust out his hand, keen to see her reaction.

She ignored his outstretched palm. 'Not out here. Too public for what I have to say. Why don't you come into my lair?'

Now, *that* was the best offer he'd had all day.

He followed her, admiring the gentle swishing of the long skirt around her ankles. She wore sandals, an anklet and a silver toe-ring, and he briefly wondered if they completed her outfit or she favoured that sort of thing all the time. He'd never been a fan of jewellery, especially the bizarre piercings that many women liked these days. In fact, he would hazard a guess that this lady sported a navel-ring to match the one wrapped around her second toe.

'Do you intend to come in or are you going to stand out there all day, admiring my feet?' She held open a purple drape and gestured him inside, a cheeky smile tugging at the corners of her lush mouth.

Lord, that mouth. Outlined in a sheer pink gloss, it sent his imagination into overdrive. The midday sun must have addled his brain more than he'd thought. Since when did he ever mix business with pleasure?

He brushed past her and entered the gloom. 'Who said I was admiring anything?'

'I see all,' she said, sitting behind a small table covered in red satin. 'So, truth time. Show me your palm.'

Feeling utterly ridiculous, and wondering what the hell he was doing in a claustrophobic tent at a run-down theme park, he reached forward and unfurled his fingers.

As soon as she touched him, he knew. This mystery woman had grabbed his attention the first minute he'd laid eyes on her and he would have followed her anywhere to find out more.

'OK, Miss Know-All. Am I an open book?'

She peered into his palm, turning it from side to side. 'Mmm…interesting.'

You can say that again.

With her attention focused on his hand, he had free rein to study her just as intently. Her veil had fallen back as she leaned forward, displaying a glorious mass of wild blonde hair which tumbled past her shoulders. She obviously spent a lot of time outdoors, her hair's sun-streaked highlights shimmered in the candlelight, framing her tanned face. A slight frown marred her forehead as she studied his palm, her mouth pursed in concentration, and he had a sudden urge to smooth away the frown and kiss those pouting lips.

She was a beauty all right. A pity he had to rush back to Sydney, otherwise he might have enjoyed getting to know her a whole lot better.

'You still haven't told me anything,' he said, wishing she would look at him so he could glimpse those startling eyes once again.

As if reading his thoughts, she looked up and

fixed him with a piercing stare. 'You're impatient, self-assured and used to getting your own way. A real go-getter, who won't let anyone stop you from reaching your goal, with a liberal dose of arrogance thrown in for good measure.'

His eyebrows shot up. 'Oh, you're good. Anything else?'

'You're nothing but trouble.' She pronounced it calmly, though he noted her hand shook before she quickly dropped his.

'Only when someone stands in my way.' Despite the fact that she piqued his interest, he glanced at his watch and decided he'd wasted enough time. He stood up, suddenly annoyed that he'd dallied this long. He needed to find Colin Lawrence and get down to business.

'Tell me something I don't know. So what do you want with Colin?' She sat back and folded her arms, as if she had all the time in the world.

He didn't. 'I'm here on business. Now, where can I find him?'

She nodded, like the all-seeing sage she pretended to be. 'I knew it. You're one of the vultures. Accountant? Lawyer?' She spat out the last word, as if the profession was poison.

He quirked an eyebrow, admiring her feistiness. 'You really do have amazing powers. My name's Steve Rockwell and I'm a lawyer, here on behalf of Water World.'

She clenched her fists, fear flashing in her eyes before she tilted her chin up.

'Go away. We've got nothing to say to you.'

'We?' Since when did a pint-sized woman posing as a fortune-teller speak for the business he'd come to close down?

She jumped to her feet. 'You heard me. My father and I aren't interested in your *business*. So go back to where you came from.'

God, she was magnificent when riled, bristling like some fierce tawny cat, her eyes glowing with golden fire. He wouldn't mind taking a shot at taming her, though she'd just thrown a major spanner in the works. This creature was Colin Lawrence's daughter and he never mixed business with pleasure.

He shook his head. 'That's not possible. Unless the owner of this establishment speaks to me and brokers a deal, this place is finished.'

She walked around the table and stood in front of him. 'No deal. That monstrosity next door has been trying to buy us out for years and it just won't happen. Got it?'

'Water World is one of the largest theme parks around here. Do you really think you stand a chance?' He towered over her, feeling like a nasty ogre come to wipe out the Lilliputians.

To his amazement, she jabbed her finger into his chest, several times. 'Now, you listen to me, mister. This place is my father's life and no one is going to take it away from him, least of all the likes of you.

What do I have to do to get it through that thick skull of yours?'

He'd never been impulsive. His whole life had been planned, from the exact minute of his C-section birth, just as his mother wanted it. In fact, every action in his well-ordered life had been planned to the nth degree.

Except what he did next.

Pulling her against him, he claimed her mouth with almost brutal force. She'd stirred him with her spirited retorts and quick wit and he needed to prove a point. Though he forgot what it was the moment his lips touched hers.

She didn't stand a chance as he kissed her like a man starved, coaxing her lips to open beneath him. She made a soft, whimpering sound before giving in, her mouth allowing his tongue to plunge between her lips, seeking, plundering. He plied her mouth with prolonged skill, nipping her bottom lip, nibbling and suckling till she leaned into him.

His fingers tangled in her hair as he angled her head for better access to the sweetness of her mouth. Like a forbidden delicacy, he tasted and sampled, accepting he would regret it later. Surprisingly, she met him halfway, grasping his shirt and hanging on for dear life as he deepened the kiss to the point of devouring. At her touch, he drew in a breath, knowing he shouldn't be doing this yet powerless to stop. He'd lost all reason the minute the temptress responded to him.

Suddenly, she pushed away from him, a dawning horror growing in her passion-hazed eyes. 'What was *that* all about?'

'I'm sorry,' he murmured, drawing back farther. He took in her flushed cheeks, her slightly swollen lips, her ragged breathing, not sorry in the least.

In fact, he wished he could kiss her again, repeatedly, till she lay writhing beneath him, begging for more.

She turned away from him and ran a hand through her tousled hair. 'I think you should leave.'

He could have sworn her voice shook, and remorse flooded him. What was he doing, going around manhandling the daughter of the man he needed to do business with? He'd never given in to primal urges before. He usually planned his seductions—not that he had any intention of following through with this particular scenario. Ladies sporting toe-rings weren't his style at all.

He reached towards her, then let his hand drop. Touching her wouldn't be a good idea at this point of the proceedings. 'What's your name?'

She whirled around and he glimpsed the fire return to her eyes. 'It's a bit late to exchange pleasantries, don't you think?'

He deserved that for acting like a first-class jerk. Though he wasn't big on apologies, he'd better make amends before she ran crying to Daddy and Colin Lawrence came after him with a shotgun. Or, even worse, a lawsuit.

He lowered his head just a fraction, aiming for humble in the hope she would buy it. He'd never acted subservient in his life and it didn't sit well with him now. 'I don't know what came over me. Please accept my apology. You just got me so wound up, I—'

'Do you kiss everyone who talks back to you?' she interrupted, crossing her arms.

Once again, his mind drifted into the gutter as he wondered if her breasts would feel as heavy and full as they looked through the gauzy material.

He shrugged, bringing his attention back to her face with difficulty. 'I'm not used to it. I don't get disagreed with all that often.'

Sensing the direction of his gaze, she folded her arms tighter and glared. 'Well, there's a first time for everything. It's about time someone took you down a peg or two and I'm just the person to do it.'

He took in her defensive stance, a flicker of appreciation shooting through him. This woman would fight to the death for what she believed in, to protect what was rightfully hers. He admired loyalty, a rare attribute in most of the women he'd had the misfortune to date.

'Be careful. I just might take you up on that challenge.' He paused, looking her up and down. 'And we both know where that might lead.'

She blushed, a faint pink staining her cheeks, highlighting the bewitching colour of her eyes. 'My father won't be back till later. I'll tell him you called in. And now, if you don't mind, I have work to do.' She held her head high and strode past him, holding open the tent flap for him to exit with her.

'You win this time. But I'll be back.' He stepped out of the tent, the sunshine momentarily blinding him and he wondered if she'd cast some weird spell on him while he'd been cocooned with her.

She looked up and he could have sworn she winked. 'I'm sure you will. See you round, hotshot.'

She sashayed away and his body responded before he realised she still hadn't answered his question. 'What's your name?' he called out.

She stopped for a moment. 'Amber,' she flung over her shoulder and continued on her way.

The name suited her. Her hair and skin were a golden bronze that more than lived up to the semi-precious stone she'd probably been named after.

What a woman.

Perhaps this deal would be more complicated than he'd thought? And, just perhaps, he'd need to spend more time on the Gold Coast than first anticipated?

Yeah, it was do-able. Though how he would justify the last half-hour as billable time was beyond him.

Amber stalked across the grounds towards her father's office, wondering what on earth had possessed her to match wits with the likes of that fancy lawyer.

She'd picked him as soon as he'd entered the carnival, striding through the crowd with his nose stuck ten feet in the air. The designer suit had been a dead give-away too, not to mention the fact that her father had warned her about some big-time lawyer from Sydney coming to pay them a visit.

OK, so he hadn't been what she'd expected. Old, wrinkly and conservative didn't come close to describing the high-and-mighty Steve Rockwell. Not by a long shot. Try thirty-ish, lean and drop-dead gorgeous.

Not that she wanted to remember him. Anything he'd had to say and that damn kiss should be pushed to the far recesses of her mind, where they belonged.

So what if he'd made her toes curl? She'd been kissed before. *But never like that.*

So maybe he had turned up enough heat to melt her on the spot. She could cope. She'd handled worse and come away unscathed. And if he thought for one minute he could undermine her stance on the carnival with a single kiss, he better think again.

She knocked once before barging into her father's makeshift office. 'Hi, Dad. Got a minute?'

Colin Lawrence looked up, pleasure etched into his weary face. He pushed his glasses on top of his balding head and leaned back in his chair. 'I've always got time for my favourite girl. What's up?'

'I just ran into that lawyer you talked about. And he's spouting a whole lot of trouble.'

Her father's worried expression made her heart clench. 'We've talked about this, love. There's no avoiding it. Where is he?'

'I fobbed him off for now, though he said he'd be back. Isn't there anything we can do? Get another loan? Re-finance?' She wanted to stamp her feet and yell at the injustice of it all.

He shook his head, sending her brief, irrational flare of hope plummeting. 'There's nothing left. I've got no choice. It's sell out to the big boys or close up.' He rubbed the bridge of his nose where his glasses had rested moments before. 'I'm sorry, darling. There just isn't any other way.'

Amber walked over to her father, bent down and hugged him. 'Don't worry, things will be OK. You'll see.' She blinked back the tears that rose at her empty promise.

Things had never been the same since her mother had died when Amber was twelve years old, after a long, expensive battle with cancer. Her father had done everything in his power to keep the carnival afloat, a lasting legacy of happier times, of a business her parents had built from scratch.

Later he'd insisted on paying her university bills, leaving their floundering finances in dire straits. So she had a business degree? Big deal. It couldn't save the carnival and it only served to increase her guilt at attributing to their monetary woes.

And now her dad would lose the one thing that meant the world to him. She'd be damned if she just stood by and let it happen.

'Why don't you meet with this lawyer and see

what he has to say?' The words stuck in her craw but she knew there was no other way.

She'd sensed a softer side beneath the arrogant lawyer's polished exterior and she hoped that he might have an ounce of decency in his supercilious bones. Anything was worth a shot at this late stage.

Her father nodded. 'I had every intention of meeting with him. Why did you shoo him away?'

She shrugged, remembering the toe-curling kiss and the feel of his rock-hard chest beneath her hands. She'd needed to get rid of him before she did something even more stupid like take him back to her caravan. 'Guess he rubbed me up the wrong way.'

Lord, if her dad only knew how she'd really reacted to the sexy lawyer and the exact way he'd rubbed her!

Her dad tweaked her nose, making her feel ten years old. 'You're too fiery for your own good, missy.'

She thrust her chin up. 'No man gets the better of me, Dad. You know that.'

He chuckled. 'Some day, some man with enough guts is going to come along and give you a mighty big shake-up. Just mark my words.'

'You're the only man in my life worth worrying about.' She squeezed his hand, trying to ignore the image of a cocky lawyer with slate-grey eyes. He did not rate a mention, let alone a passing thought.

Now all she had to do was believe it.

*　　*　　*

Before leaving the carnival, Steve decided to take a look around. He prided himself on being prepared for every deal he handled, and in this instance he didn't think that reading a bunch of reports would cut it.

He'd taken on this deal for his boss, Jeff Byrne. Jeff knew the owner of the large theme park next door, Water World, who had called in a favour and requested that Byrne and Associates represent his company in the takeover of an 'insignificant' competitor.

So here he was on the Gold Coast, keen to finalise matters and return to his harbour-side apartment, his yacht and his latest conquest, all waiting for him in civilised Sydney. He'd never liked the glitz of the Gold Coast, preferring the class of a large city.

As if on cue, he caught sight of Amber's gypsy-clad figure in the crowd, reminding him of some of the coast's hidden attractions. As she stopped to re-capture a stray balloon for some children, he watched the way the sun glinted off the blonde mane that hung halfway down her back.

OK, so the Gold Coast wasn't all bad.

She looked up as he approached her, her expression far from welcoming. 'What are you still doing here?'

'Thought I'd take a look around.'

'Why? Moving in for the kill?' She thrust her chin up as if daring him to argue.

Though he'd enjoyed their war of words earlier,

he decided to cut her some slack. After all, he'd probably feel the same way if someone threatened to take away his livelihood. 'I'm here to broker a deal. That's it.'

'Do you have any idea what this place means to us?' Her eyes narrowed and she blinked several times, quickly.

He caught the sheen in her eyes. Surely he hadn't made the firebrand cry?

'Why don't you show me?' Great, he'd gone soft for the second time in his life.

The only other time he'd relented was when one of his exes, Kara Roberts, had come crying on his shoulder about her boyfriend, Matt Byrne, his one-time rival and current associate. Women's tears left him helpless and uncomfortable, two feelings that didn't sit well with him. It had been an experience he didn't care to repeat.

So what was he doing, playing knight-in-shining-armour all over again to a woman he barely knew?

The glimmer of her smile was answer enough.

'Sure you want the grand tour?' she asked, her voice still a tad unsteady.

He inclined his head. 'Lead the way.'

He traipsed after her, listening to the pride in her running commentary as she outlined the carnival's features. Surprisingly, the operation ran more smoothly than he'd anticipated and the happiness on the employees' faces seemed genuine enough. So why wasn't it turning a profit? Did Colin Lawrence have a gambling habit, or some other way of losing money in what appeared like a sound business?

'Why are you in trouble?' He'd brokered deals for worse places than this. Maybe something could be salvaged from the operation? And, in the process, stop his enchanting tour guide from staring at him as if he was a bogeyman.

She sighed as her shoulders tensed. 'We ran up a debt a few years ago and haven't been able to recover since. Things have gone from bad to worse since the big boys joined the party.'

'You mean the other theme parks around here?' He knew of at least three major parks in the area that drew the crowds in droves with their huge marketing campaigns.

She nodded. 'Though we pride ourselves on old-fashioned quality, it just isn't enough any more. We can't afford to give away cars or free trips to our customers. All we can do is provide kids with a carnival experience, like days gone by.'

He glanced around, noting the merry-go-round, with its restored hand-painted horses, the apple bobbing, the food vendors selling candy floss and hot dogs. She was right; he'd never seen a place like this except in the movies. And he'd come to tear it all down.

'Is there any way of saving it?'

'We've tried everything.' She turned away from him and he glimpsed a gleam of tears again. 'What do you care anyway? You're on *their* side.' She gestured to her right, where he could just see a monstrous water slide over the treetops.

He'd been accused of many things in his lifetime, mostly by his opposition on deals they had lost. None of the barbs or insults he'd had to put up with in the past came close to affecting him as much as this woman's inference that he was here to rip her world apart.

'I'm not taking sides. I'm just doing my job.' He spoke the truth, so why did it sound so lame?

She started to walk away and waved her hand in a dismissive gesture. 'Whatever lets you sleep at night.'

He strode after her, grabbed her arm and swung her around to face him. 'Look, if there's anything I can do to help, just let me know.'

What was he doing, co-operating with the little league when he'd come here to play hard ball?

She leaned into him, and for one irrational minute he thought she might kiss him. 'There is something you can do for me.'

He inhaled, savouring the sandalwood fragrance that drifted up from her nearness. He'd smelled something similar earlier, thinking it was the incense burning in a corner of the tent. Now, her scent wrapped around him like an ancient spell, one he couldn't resist.

'What is it?' He refrained from saying he would do anything for her. In fact, he would walk over hot coals for another taste of her delicious mouth.

She stared directly at him, that already too-familiar fire flashing in her eyes. 'Get lost.'

In an instant she'd wrenched her arm free of his grip and stalked away, head held high.

He willed her to look back but she didn't. Too bad. He wanted her to see his smug grin.

If there was one thing he loved more than making money it was a challenge, and the feisty Amber Lawrence had just waved a red cape, leaving him pawing the ground in frustration and ready to charge.

CHAPTER TWO

AMBER believed in karma. If you treated others badly, it would come back to you tenfold. Now, after the way she'd spoken to Steve Rockwell earlier, she had her comeuppance.

'Are you sure you can't make the meeting, Dad?' She tugged at the hem of her skirt, feeling more than a tad self-conscious in the mini cocktail dress.

'I'm sorry, love. If I go out this headache is sure to turn into a full-blown migraine. Besides, you can handle it. You're my right-hand woman.' He winked at her, though it turned into a wince as he lay back on the bed and rubbed his temples.

'I know, but you're the one who needs to make the final decision.' The skirt wouldn't co-operate and rode halfway up her thighs as soon as she let go. It had been too long since she'd bought any clothes, not that it usually mattered. However, with a meeting this important she wanted to look her best and unfortunately the three-year-old dress had seen better days.

'Just listen to what he has to say,' her dad continued. 'You don't need to agree on anything immediately. We'll discuss it in the morning, OK?'

Guilt flooded her as he closed his eyes. Why was

she making such a big deal out of a meeting she could handle with one hand tied behind her back?

Because it wasn't so much the dinner meeting her dad had scheduled that was the problem but the man she had to share the meal with.

'Besides, Mr Rockwell sounded quite reasonable over the phone. I'm sure you two will get along just fine.'

She leaned down and kissed her dad on the cheek, hoping he was right. 'Don't worry about a thing. I'll let you know how it went in the morning. And don't forget, ring me if you need me.'

He waved her away. 'Stop fussing. I just need to sleep.'

As she looked down upon her father's leather-worn face as he drifted off to sleep, her heart swelled with love. He'd given her the best life possible, nurturing and protecting her throughout the vulnerable teenage years after her mum had passed away. She couldn't have wished for a better father, and the least she could do was put up with an obnoxious lawyer for one evening.

She tiptoed from the room and wondered where the meeting would take place. She hadn't eaten out for ages, not since her last date six months ago. There hadn't been much time for dating lately, with all her attention focused on saving the business. Besides, the local guys just didn't do it for her.

A loud knock on the door set her nerves jumping. Checking her reflection in the mirror one last time, she wished that she'd done more with her face. She didn't wear much make-up as a rule, and the lack of cosmetics made her look too young. Tonight she needed a mask of confidence.

She fixed a welcoming smile on her face and opened the door. 'Hello.'

She couldn't think of anything else to say, especially when the last words she'd uttered to this guy were 'get lost'. To make matters worse, he looked amazing, clad in black trousers and a white shirt unbuttoned at the neck. Casual, yet smart, and, combined with his lethal looks, way too dangerous for her.

'Ready to go?' His gaze swept her from head to foot and she had a sudden urge to slam the door in his face and dive under a duvet, especially when he focused on her legs.

'Sure.' *That was one way to impress him, blind him with riveting conversation.*

She gnawed at her bottom lip, wishing she could think of something to say, and followed him to the carnival's entrance, where people queued for the evening's performance. Unfortunately, the paltry line would barely pay the overheads in staging the horse show. Just another nail in the coffin.

'I've hired a car for a couple of days. It's this way.' She watched him stride towards a low-slung convertible, admiring his long legs and tight butt.

He held the passenger door open for her and she slid into the seat, wondering how many other women he'd tried to impress with his gallant behaviour. Somehow, the thought of him wining and dining countless other women didn't improve her mood. Not that she should care. Tonight was business, and the sooner she believed it, the better.

'Figures,' she said, settling into the comfortable leather seat and watching his long legs fold underneath the steering wheel.

'Pardon?' He started the car and pulled away from the kerb, his attention focused on the road ahead.

Thank goodness he'd stopped staring at her. She couldn't stand the way he'd looked at her as she sat down, probably wondering where she'd picked up the ridiculously short dress and why she was wearing it to an important meeting.

'The car. It fits.'

'Are you judging me?' His voice was low, a warning that she trod on uneven ground.

'So what if I am?' *Where had that come from?* She was here to save her dad's business, not shoot it down in flames.

'You've got a smart mouth for a woman in no position to bait me. I'm supposed to be the bad guy, remember?'

She tossed back her hair, wishing she'd had the sense to wear it up. How would she look by the time they made it to the restaurant after riding in an open-top? So much for appearing professional.

Rather than backing down, she had a strange urge to match wits with him. 'I've never kowtowed to any guy and I'm not about to start now, regardless of who you are.'

'Trying to pick a fight with me won't work,' he said, hitting a button on the CD-player.

In doing so, his fingers grazed her bare leg and she flinched, unprepared for the swift rush of longing for his hand to do a lot more than just brush against her. What was going on? She'd never reacted to a guy like this, especially one whose head would barely pass through an average-sized doorway.

Serene rainforest sounds filled the car, in stark contrast to her simmering mood, and she wondered why an uptight lawyer would listen to music like this. Why did he annoy her so much? All he had to do was open his mouth and she aimed for his throat, wishing she could tear it out with her bare hands.

'That's better,' she murmured, appreciating the soothing music. She meditated daily to a similar track, and its familiarity evoked an instant sense of calm.

'You like this stuff?'

She glanced across at him, noting the incredulity on his face. 'Of course. It keeps me centred.'

'Whatever that means.'

She chuckled. 'Something you'll never figure out. Though you've surprised me. I thought your musical tastes would run more towards Bach...Mozart... You know, boring classical stuff.'

'Still judging me, huh?' He sounded amused

rather than annoyed. 'The CD came with the car. Oh, and in case you're interested, I happen to prefer pop to classical stuff.'

Somehow, she couldn't imagine him bopping along to the latest beat and the thought made her smile. 'I'm not interested. I'm only here to have dinner with you in the hope we can save the carnival.'

'Speaking of dinner, let me guess. You're a vegetarian too?'

'And what's wrong with that?' She folded her arms, enjoying their banter yet wishing he would stop pushing her buttons.

'Nothing. I should've asked before booking the restaurant. Sorry.' Rather than sounding apologetic, he spoke like a man used to having his own way and expecting everyone around him to fit in.

Her theatrical gasp overrode the muted bird sounds filtering from the speakers. 'Was that an apology? I must be hearing things.'

'Ha ha. A regular comedienne. Is there any end to your many talents?'

'You'll just have to wait and see.' She averted her gaze from his strong hands splayed across the steering wheel and glanced out of the window in time to see the giant conglomerate that was trying to ruin her father's business. Though she'd loved water slides as a child, she hated the way Water World had ruined the environment with its plastic monstrosities, rather than blending the park into the bush

surrounds. And now they wanted to expand, bull-
dozing another part of the bush and her father's
business in the process.

She sneaked a peek at the man who had the power
to make it all happen. Though it went against the
grain, perhaps she should be nice to him rather than
antagonise him further?

'I'm not a vegetarian,' she ventured, thinking the
statement lacked something as a peace offering but
not wanting to give in to him too easily. 'So when
do we start discussing the carnival?'

'I don't talk business on an empty stomach,' he
said as he drove into Surfers Paradise and handed
over the car to be valet-parked. Amber didn't reply,
and as she climbed out of the car she hoped that he
didn't expect her to make polite conversation over
dinner. All she wanted to do was get this business
completed as quickly as possible without compli-
cating matters.

For that was exactly what would happen if she
spent too long in this guy's company. She'd never
met a man like him and he intrigued her, the way
he wouldn't back down. Usually, her forthright man-
ner scared men off, but not this one. He seemed to
thrive on it, a fact she liked way too much to be
comfortable.

'Hope you like seafood,' he said as he guided her
into a prominent Gold Coast hotel.

'I love it,' she responded, trying not to gawk at
the elaborate foyer, with its huge crystal chandelier

casting a muted glow over the cream and gold furnishings. Well-dressed patrons strolled through the
lobby, some heading to the restaurant.

'Be careful. Sounds like you might actually enjoy
this evening.' His teasing words did little to reassure
her as she compared the elegant styles of the other
ladies with her own out-of-date dress. She didn't
belong here, and the sooner she escaped, the better.

'What's wrong?' He laid a hand on her arm and
she found his touch strangely comforting.

She glanced down at her dress, feeling like
Cinderella without the fairy godmother and twice as
ugly as the stepsisters. 'I don't fit in.'

He placed his thumb under her chin and tilted her
head up. 'You look beautiful.' His eyes darkened to
pewter and sent her pulse-rate accelerating at a
frightening speed. Though she knew she didn't look
it at that moment, she felt like a princess.

Desire skittered across her nerve-endings as his
thumb wandered up to lightly brush her bottom lip.

'In fact, you're the most stunning woman in this
room. Now let's order.'

They followed the *maître d'* to a cosy table for
two, shaded from the other diners by strategically
placed palms. It overlooked the ocean, and the twin-
kling lights of the Surfers Paradise strip created the
illusion of being suspended in air.

This, combined with his compliment, which had
rendered her speechless, meant she could scarcely
concentrate on the menu.

'See anything you fancy?'

She looked up, biting back her first response concerning the man sitting opposite. 'I'll have the king prawns, please.'

'Excellent choice.' He placed their order with the waiter and handed her one of the delicate flutes that had just been filled. 'How about champagne to celebrate?'

He must be buttering her up for something, but she couldn't figure out what. 'To celebrate?'

He clinked glasses with hers. 'To the start of a long and prosperous relationship.'

'For who?'

'Both of us.'

She almost choked as the effervescent bubbles tingled down her throat. She had no idea how closing down her family business could benefit him, or result in a long relationship, but she had an inkling she was about to find out.

'Tell me how you'd save the business.' He sat back and folded his arms, a curious look on his face.

She ignored the flare of hope, knowing his interest was purely speculative. 'We need more capital to pay off our existing debts. Once they're cleared, I have a few marketing ideas to boost business. We still have our regulars plus the tourists, and I know I can increase the profits.'

'What makes you so sure?'

She didn't let his intense scrutiny unnerve her. 'I took marketing as part of my business degree. I have a few tricks up my sleeve, but unless we clear the debts we'll go under.'

'*You've* got a business degree?' His eyebrows shot heavenward and his mouth dropped open, just like one of the sideshow clowns at the carnival. A pity she didn't have any Ping-Pong balls handy to shove into his gaping mouth.

She bristled. 'With honours. Why, did you think I was just another carnival hick?'

His lips twitched and he avoided her stare, focusing on refolding his linen napkin. 'I just didn't pick you to be the type.'

Oh-oh, now he was treading on dangerous ground. She hated being labelled in any way, shape or form.

'And what type is that? Uptight, stuck-up, pretentious, like you?'

He shrugged, as if her barbs meant little. 'I'm proud of what I am. At least I don't have some hang-up over wealth.'

Anger surged through her. Easy for him to judge, when he obviously had money to burn.

'Not that it's any of your business, but you wouldn't know the first thing about making it in this world the hard way. That is, without Daddy's purse strings to tide you over.' She barely paused for breath, her bitterness rising with every passing second as she ticked the list off on her fingers. 'Let me guess. You went to private schools, graduated from university top of the class, had the weekend beach house, played golf with Daddy and dated the princesses hand-picked by Mummy. Correct?'

Her tirade had a strange effect, but he blanked all expression from his face, casually picked up his glass and drank as if she hadn't spoken.

'Like I've said before, your clairvoyant skills amaze me. You left out the yacht, though.' His deadly calm unnerved her, though he didn't look up.

Her anger deflated, gone as quickly as it had come as guilt flooded her. She shouldn't have pushed him so far. She was here to broker a salvage operation, not blow the whole thing out of the water. 'Look, you don't know the first thing about me. I just don't like being put inside a box.'

'Then tell me.' He leaned forward and rested his forearms on the table, drawing her attention to the way his shirt moulded to his biceps. He had a great body for an office-based guy. 'What makes Amber Lawrence tick?'

She squirmed, uncomfortable beneath his probing gaze. 'I'm a free spirit. I love Nepalese food, bush-walking and exquisite Mexican jewellery. Not that I own any of the latter yet. And, as you probably noticed, my taste in clothes is far from the usual. There, does that satisfy you?'

Interest flared in his eyes as his gaze swept her body, sending her heart hammering. 'On the contrary. It *arouses* my curiosity further.'

She blinked to break the hypnotising eye contact,

imagining the many ways she could arouse him and vice versa.

Thankfully, the arrival of their meal put paid to any further interrogation and Amber breathed a sigh of relief. This man had the power to twist her into knots and she had no idea how to untangle herself. The sooner he laid his cards on the table and left her alone, the better.

Once she'd finished the last of her delicious prawns smothered in garlic and chilli, she sat back and patted her stomach. 'That was fantastic.'

Her action drew his stare to that region of her anatomy like a magnet and she quickly sat up, disconcerted at the heat that unravelled in her belly and spread to lower regions.

'Can I tempt you with dessert?' His low, husky voice sent a shiver of anticipation down her spine.

That depends. Are you offering dessert…or dessert?

By the amused look on his face, she thought for a sudden, horrifying moment that she'd spoken aloud.

'No, thanks.' She clasped her hands tightly, wishing the evening would come to an end.

'Sweet enough, huh?'

She looked up at him from beneath her lashes, wishing her heart would stop pounding. She knew she shouldn't flirt with him but a little incorrigible voice inside her head wouldn't accept that. 'You tell me.'

'I'd say you're something like a lemon tart. Looks delicious but with a tang that can set you on edge.' Unfortunately, he kept staring at her with blatant hunger, as if he had every intention of sampling her and coming back for seconds.

'Yeah, well, you'll never get a taste.'

At the speculative gleam in his eyes, she cleared her throat and continued quickly, 'Thanks for the meal. Now, back to business. I've told you my ideas. What do you think?'

He hadn't discussed much about the proposed takeover at all. In fact, he'd focused far too much attention on her, and not the business they had come here to talk about.

'Don't worry. I'll be over to see your father first thing in the morning.' He spoke calmly, rationally, but she sensed something more. If she wasn't mistaken, he sounded like a chauvinistic male who thought deals could only be sealed between men.

She pushed back her chair and stood up so quickly her head spun. She couldn't believe he'd sidetracked her with good food, fine champagne and diverse conversation. And now, when she needed some concrete information to take home, he was giving her the brush-off.

'I do have half a brain in my head, so if you decide to do business, let me know. I'll be waiting outside.' Resisting the urge to tug down her skirt and spoil her exit, she stalked out of the dining room, head held high.

Steve watched her walk away, the green dress she wore flouncing against her thighs. He couldn't believe she'd worn a dress that short, especially after the kiss they had shared. What did she think he was, made of stone?

Unfortunately, a certain part of his anatomy had thought so since the minute he laid eyes on her tonight. Her body was every bit as luscious as he'd imagined, and thankfully had been on full display since the disappearance of that ridiculous gypsy-like outfit she'd worn earlier that afternoon.

Admit it, Rockwell. She has you hooked.

Pushing the niggling thought from his head, he paid the bill and followed her outside. She'd wandered towards the beach, where the wind whipped her hair back and plastered the flimsy dress against her shapely legs.

'Unless you want to get arrested for indecent exposure, I suggest you get in the car,' he murmured in her ear, catching a tantalising glimpse of cleavage as she whirled around.

'Stop telling me what to do. And don't sneak up on me like that.' She spoke quietly, but he sensed the barely restrained anger beneath her calm exterior.

He offered her an arm. 'Have I done something to offend you?'

She stared at his arm as if he had some contagious disease. 'What haven't you done? You waltz into our lives, ready to close down a family business.

Then you bring me out here to supposedly discuss the aforementioned, yet don't. And as for that kiss...' She trailed off and looked away.

He took a step closer, bringing him within a foot of her. 'I'm not going to apologise again for something I don't regret.'

That got her attention, and her gaze flew to his face. Thankfully, he managed to maintain a cool façade while his gut twisted with desire. If she kept staring at him with those eyes he wouldn't be responsible for his actions, and this time there would be no stopping him.

'Let's go.' She turned around and stalked towards the car, leaving him with a distinct case of lust that he needed to ignore.

She didn't speak a word on the trip back to the carnival, pointedly staring out of the passenger window. He sneaked a peek at her, wondering what it was about this strange woman that appealed to him so much. Usually he preferred tall, cool brunettes, not wild blondes with sharp tongues.

She'd surprised him with her business degree. He couldn't imagine her stalking the corridors of power, though he would bet she'd put anyone who crossed her path back into line, quick smart. And as for her tastes, he should have guessed they would match the rest of her: alternative, exotic, fascinating.

She intrigued him. He wondered how long he could string out this deal with her father. Hopefully at least till he'd sampled the hidden delights of this rare woman.

She practically bolted from the car as he pulled up outside the carnival and shut off the engine.

'Hey, wait up.' He strode after her, his long strides eating up the ground, her high heels no match for them. He caught her at the Ferris wheel.

'Goodnight. See you in the morning.' Her gaze flickered past him and a huge smile lit up her face. 'Time to pack it in, Stan?'

Wishing that special smile was for him, he turned and saw a wizened old man doffing a moth-eaten hat that had seen better days. 'Evenin', miss. Yeah, it's about that time.'

Steve looked back at her and raised an eyebrow, angling for an introduction. She got the message. 'Stan, I'd like you to meet Steve Rockwell.'

Stan thrust out a hand. 'Pleased to meet ya. Any lad of this young lady is a friend of mine.'

Steve stifled a grin and shook the old guy's hand, not daring to look at Amber.

'Oh, he's not my lad, Stan. He's just a—' She bit back what she'd been about to say and he knew why. If the carnival was about to close down, she wouldn't want the employees to know a lawyer was sniffing around.

He stepped in quickly. 'An old friend.'

She cast him a grateful look and he pushed home his momentary advantage. 'I've never been for a ride on one of these, you know.'

She frowned as Stan immediately took Steve's hint. 'Well, then, sir, hop aboard. Nothing like it in the world when you're up the top, swaying in the breeze, holding onto your sweetheart's hand.' Stan winked as he opened a side-door to one of the chairs.

Steve could have sworn he heard Amber snort as he grabbed her hand and pulled her with him. 'Come on, *sweetheart*. It'll be fun.'

'Oh, yeah, a real barrel of laughs.' She tugged free of his hand but followed him in.

He hadn't lied when he'd said he'd never been on a Ferris wheel before. If he'd known how snug the seats were he'd have taken all his girlfriends for a ride.

With Amber's thigh pressed against his and her signature scent enveloping him, he knew this was the best idea he'd had in a long time.

'You could have set the record straight with Stan.'

'What? And disillusion the old guy? Have a heart.'

She tried to shift away from him, which set the chair swinging. 'He's not used to me bringing guys around.'

He slid an arm around her shoulders, surprised yet thankful she didn't shrug it off. 'A girl like you should have men falling at her feet. Why don't you bring any of them home?'

'They're not important enough.'

Jealousy stabbed at his gut, swift and sharp, at the

thought of Amber with other men. Ludicrous, as he'd known her for less than twenty-four hours. He pushed his luck. 'Ever been on a ride with any of them before?'

She turned to face him and his heart pounded, a totally irrational response from an organ he controlled with precision when it came to the fairer sex.

'This is a first.' Her soft words were whipped away by the wind as the wheel slowed and finally stopped, leaving them perched at the top.

However, he didn't have time to appreciate the view when a gorgeous woman like Amber stared up at him with a mouth just begging to be kissed.

'Don't you just love new experiences?' he murmured, as he brushed her lips in a feather-light kiss.

A light sigh escaped her lips as they parted. He nibbled her bottom lip before easing his tongue into her mouth, challenging her to match him thrust for thrust. She didn't disappoint and their tongues duelled, firing his rising passion to new heights. As she returned his kiss all sense fled. He shouldn't be doing this. She was the daughter of the opposition, she was trouble, she was business. However, as she moaned, all he could think about was the sheer, unadulterated pleasure of her delicious mouth flowering under his.

He cupped one hand behind her neck, drawing her closer, deepening the kiss with possessive thoroughness. She tasted tart and sweet, just as he'd anticipated, and he couldn't get enough of her. He'd never understood the crazy, head-over-heels physical-attraction thing, preferring to choose his women with calculated precision for what they could do for him rather than acting on lustful impulse. Until now.

Amber's fingers tangled in his hair, pulling him closer as she arched towards him. God, she was practically offering herself to him, and he couldn't do much more than kiss her, perched this far off the ground. He would give anything for a bed right about now.

Before he could think, his free hand slid up her bare thigh, as it had itched to do all night, creating a trail of tiny goose-bumps beneath his touch.

'Whoa!' She pulled away as his hand almost reached its target.

He stared at her, not moving an inch.

'I think this belongs to you.' She grasped his wayward hand and placed it firmly in his lap before tugging her skirt down. 'Time to go down.'

'Thought you'd never offer,' he mumbled, turning away from her and staring at the distant twinkle of city lights illuminating the horizon, wishing for a fickle wind to flip the flimsy skirt she wore. Every time she'd reached for the skirt-edge during the evening he'd wanted to still her hand, hoping it would ride up farther.

She stiffened beside him but didn't reply. At that moment the wheel started up again and they drifted back down to earth in silence.

She bolted from the chair as soon as Stan raised the bar.

'Thanks, Stan. It was great.' He shook the old man's hand.

'I'm sure it was, Mr Rockwell. See ya round.' They grinned like co-conspirators before Steve took off after Amber.

He always seemed to be chasing after her—something he never did with women. Usually they trailed after him, impressed by his wealth and status. So what was it about this woman that had him running around in circles?

She stopped as he grabbed her arm. 'I'll see you in the morning?'

'Not if I can help it.' She glared at him, gold flecks glinting in the moonlight.

'It was just a kiss, dammit. Don't get so wound up.'

'Who says I'm wound up?' She backed away from him ever so slightly.

He loved her defiance, etched into every aspect of her body language. 'You're tighter than a coiled spring ready to snap.'

'And you're a lousy judge of character. Goodnight.' She spun on her heel and stalked away.

He pondered her parting jibe. Contrary to her opinion, one of his greatest skills was reading people and their motives. And he was damn good at it too. Then why hadn't he figured her out yet?

'Pleasant dreams,' he called out, already looking

forward to the next day, eager to match wits once again with the enchanting Amber.

She ignored him, a relatively novel experience for his ego.

He chuckled, aiming to change all that, starting first thing in the morning.

CHAPTER THREE

As soon as Steve entered his hotel room he noticed the red blinking light on the phone, indicating he had a message. Perhaps it was Amber, giving him another serve before she went to bed?

Surprisingly, it was his mother, urging him to call as soon as possible, regardless of the time. He dialled the number, not in the mood for one of his mother's famous tirades. What had he done or not done this time?

She answered on the first ring. 'Darling. Where have you been? I've been trying to get hold of you all evening.'

'Business, Mother. You know, that thing I do for a living?'

He heard a sniff and imagined the disdainful expression on his mother's well-preserved face. 'Don't bait me, darling. You know you don't have to work. It's just some perverse streak that pushes you to earn a living when you're more than comfortable.'

Georgia Rockwell, queen of the understatement. His mother's version of 'comfortable' meant filthy, stinking rich, a fact he'd been only too aware of his entire life. She'd never understood his ambition to be self-made, to spend his hours grappling with complex problems in order to feel some degree of achievement.

No use trying to convince her now, he'd wasted enough breath in the past. 'What did you want, Mother?'

She sighed, a superficial sound she'd used many times over the years to coerce him into doing something he didn't want to do. 'Your grandmother's condition is progressively worsening. I just thought you should know.'

A strange hollowness filled his heart at the thought of the delicate old woman, who had been the only person to show him any real love growing up, lying helpless in bed, eaten away by cancer.

'How bad is she?'

'The doctors only give her another few months at the most.'

Panic gripped him. He'd made a promise to Ethel St John when she'd first been diagnosed and unfortunately had yet to follow through. She'd said it was the one thing sustaining her, the thought of him marrying and bearing an heir for her fortune. That was one thing they particularly shared, a lack of confidence in his society mother, who would squander the money rather than fulfil a dying lady's wishes.

His mother's next words made him sit down. 'She told me, Steven.'

'Told you what?' Surely his grandmother hadn't confided in the daughter she despised?

'About your promise. So what are you doing about it?'

He proceeded with caution. His mother hadn't mentioned the money and he found that unusual. If she'd known about the stipulation in Ethel's will she would have been screaming into the receiver rather than speaking in the cultivated *sotto voce* he'd grown to hate. 'What do you mean?'

'Stop answering my questions with questions. You know perfectly well what I'm talking about. Mother informed me that the only reason she's fighting this nasty disease is to see you married. Well?'

Her short, clipped tones reminded him of endless criticisms of days gone by. 'Steven, don't talk with your mouth full. Don't run inside. Don't speak like a commoner. Don't let me catch you playing with that little tramp from next door...' It had continued throughout his childhood, a never-ending nightmare.

He grimaced, pushing the memories away. Thankfully, his grandmother hadn't divulged the whole secret. Otherwise his mother would be even more insufferable, if that were possible. 'I have everything under control, Mother. Nothing for you to worry about.'

'But I do worry, darling.'

Yeah, over who has the bigger Mercedes, the newest Gucci handbag or the largest portfolio. His mother hadn't worried about her son, ever.

'Leave it alone.' He unfurled his fingers, not realising he'd clenched his fists. 'Send my love to Gran and tell her I'll see her soon.'

'Oh, Steven.' How she managed to instill so much disapproval into those two words he would never know.

'Goodbye, Mother.' He hung up without waiting for a reply, wondering how she managed to push his buttons every time.

As he undressed, he recalled the last few months, when he'd dated what he termed 'suitable women' for his venture. For that was what marriage would be to him—a joint merging of two people, profitable to them both. However, he had standards, and he'd found most of the women lacking. Besides, bearing a child would be part of the deal, a fact that most of the women in his world would go to any lengths to avoid.

In the meanwhile, his grandmother was dying and he couldn't let her down. He wouldn't.

Suddenly, a glimmer of an idea insinuated its way into his tired brain. This marriage needed to happen quickly and it had to be a win-win situation for both parties. He needed a woman who would understand the terms of their agreement, yet fire his imagination at the same time.

Luckily, he'd just met the perfect candidate.

Short of listening in at the keyhole, Amber had no other option but to wait till her father's meeting with Steve concluded to hear the outcome. She paced the grounds, supervising the new pirate-ship ride and exchanging banter with some of the operators. Most of the carnival workers had been here for years, and she marvelled at their loyalty in the face of lucrative offers from the 'big boys' down the road.

She owed them a lot. If only there was something she could do to stave off the inevitable.

'What happened to the fortune-teller outfit?'

She jumped, unaware that the man whose image had kept her up all night had sneaked up behind her.

'I was filling in yesterday. So how did the meeting go?' She didn't have time for small talk. Her feet itched to run straight to her father and hear the news from a loved one rather than this smooth lawyer whose kisses had ensured that she tossed and turned all night.

He grinned, flashing the cocky smile that caused her treacherous heart to lurch every time. 'So all that stuff you told me was guess-work? Nice going. And here I was, thinking you had a gift.'

She didn't have time for his teasing. 'Tell me what happened. Now.'

He folded his arms and drummed his fingers, as if he had all the time in the world to make her squirm. 'Are you always this obnoxious or is it just me?'

If she'd been the dramatic type she would have slapped the infuriating smirk off his recently shaven face. Instead, she settled for words. 'It's you. Now, if you can manage to dismount from that incredibly tall horse you seem to be stuck on, and wipe that look off your face, I might actually get some answers.'

To her fury, he laughed. Rather than being chastised, he found her amusing.

'I'll tell you everything if you come for a ride with me.'

'You're joking!'

By his sudden seriousness, she knew he wasn't. 'I have a proposition for you. One that I'm sure you'll find interesting.'

She'd had enough of this. 'I doubt that. I'm going to find my father now, and I suggest you leave.'

'What I have to say could save the carnival.' He turned and walked away, leaving her gaping.

She'd never run after a man in her life. But he'd dangled in front of her the one carrot guaranteed to make her nibble. Swallowing her pride, she called out, 'I'll come with you on the damn ride. But this had better be good.'

She quickly focussed her attention on his face as he turned around. That was all she needed, for him to catch her staring at his butt. He had enough attitude already, without her infatuation compounding the problem.

His knowing grin did little to soothe her already frazzled nerves. 'Trust me.'

He might as well have asked her to bungee-jump from the Sydney Harbour Bridge but what choice did she have? If she could do anything to save her father's business she would, even if it involved smarming up to the likes of Steve Rockwell.

Half an hour later, she couldn't believe how a guy could splash money around like Steve. The hire car, the dinner and now this. When she'd accepted his offer for a ride, she hadn't quite expected a cruise up a canal on some fancy boat he'd hired.

'This is nice.' She'd never sailed on the canals, though she'd lived in Queensland her entire life. Trying not to ogle, she took in the impressive mansions lining the shores, each palatial home boasting its own private landing dock and accompanying boat. An easy life for some.

'Careful.' Steve handed her a glass of chilled chardonnay. 'That almost sounded like a compliment.'

She sipped the wine, enjoying the icy bite of the Barossa grapes. 'I call it as I see it.'

'Does that philosophy extend to all areas of your life?' He sat next to her in the bow of the boat, a little too close for comfort. Heck, if his sexy body was anywhere within five feet of her, it was too close.

'Sure does. I've never understood people who talk in riddles. Why hide behind words when the plain-spoken truth is so much better?'

He nodded, and she noticed the way the sun glinted off his dark blond hair, curling at the collar of his polo shirt. He wore it just slightly too long to be professional, a fact that surprised her. She'd picked him to be a total conformist, a man who bowed to the pressures of society. Maybe he could lighten up when needed?

Taking in his immaculately pressed khakis, the designer emblem on his polo shirt and the clearly expensive Italian deck shoes, she seriously doubted it.

'I happen to agree, though the truth can often hurt,' he said, looking at the horizon behind her, not quite meeting her eyes.

She wondered what or who had caused the momentary pain she'd seen flicker across his face. 'Only if you let it,' she replied, resisting the urge to reach up and smooth the slight frown that marred his forehead.

'Well, it's a bit hard to ignore when it's hitting you in the face every day.'

She had no idea what he was talking about, and decided that silence would be the best course of action at this point. If he needed to unburden some great, dark secret before they discussed the carnival, so be it.

He drained the rest of his wine before continuing. 'Have you ever felt so stifled that you'd do anything to run away?'

She shook her head. 'Not really. I've led a pretty charmed life. My parents let me make my own decisions from an early age. I've never felt restricted in any way, though the grief when my mum died was overwhelming. I did feel a tad stifled then.'

'How did she die?'

She sighed, amazed at the stab of pain after all these years. Her mum had been a kindred soul, a child of the hippy era who had instilled her gift of peace into Amber at an early age. She'd even been named after her mum's favourite stone.

'Cancer. A long battle.'

She noted the sudden tightening of his body, the rigidity of his neck muscles. 'My gran's dying of cancer at the moment.' He spoke so softly she barely heard.

'Oh, I'm sorry.' She reached out instinctively, knowing that words were inadequate at a time like this and hoping her touch would soothe. She believed in Reiki, and the healing power of hands, not that she would let him know that. He would probably jump overboard, thinking she was a fruitcake.

He didn't remove his hand from under hers and she longed to stroke her thumb over the back of it. 'It's an awful disease. I just feel so helpless. There's nothing I can do.'

'You must love your gran very much.'

He nodded, and she watched a hint of a smile curve his mouth upwards. 'She's the best. When I was growing up she was the only one who gave me any semblance of normality. My father was too busy making money and Mother was too busy spending it. Gran accepted me for who I was, not someone she expected me to be. She encouraged me to become a lawyer and follow my own path, understanding my need to prove myself.'

'Sounds like a remarkable woman.' Remorse tugged at her conscience for her harsh judgement yesterday. She'd accused him of being a man living off the wealth of his family, yet he seemed to despise doing just that, if his comments regarding his parents were any indication. Time to make amends. 'I think you take after her.'

He looked up, fixing her with those striking grey eyes that seemed to reflect the overcast sky. 'Was that another compliment? Careful, you might break your own record.'

She smiled, relieved that she'd lightened the moment. 'Who knows? I might go all the way and say I'm actually enjoying your company.'

'Oh, I'm hoping you'll go all the way.' The swift change in his tone, combined with the blatant desire in his eyes, startled her.

She jumped up and turned away, leaning on the railing. 'So what's this grand plan you have for saving the carnival?'

Her breath caught as he came up behind her and spread his arms either side of hers, effectively trapping her. Heat radiated from his body, setting her nerve-endings alight as she struggled to maintain composure.

'Is there anyone special in your life?' he whispered, his warm breath caressing her ear as goosebumps peppered her skin.

What kind of a girl did he think she was? Surely she wouldn't have responded to his kisses, twice in the same day, if she'd been involved with anybody. 'N-no,' she managed to stammer, and he leaned closer, almost pinning her to the rail.

'Would you like there to be?' His arms brushed hers, the light smattering of hair rasping across her skin as her pulse raised another notch.

'Depends who's offering.' She wished she could turn around and read the expression in his eyes. Was he serious or just toying with her inexperience? Not that it mattered. She could never get involved with a fancy-schmancy lawyer. Their worlds were too different, not taking into account the fact that he'd come along to turn hers upside-down.

'What if I could offer you everything you've ever desired?'

She battled the urge to whirl around as he finally touched her, his thumb tracing lazy circles on the back of her hand, which held the railing so hard that her knuckles stood out.

'Money means nothing to me,' she bit out as he covered her hands with his, fingers intertwined.

'Who said anything about money?' He kissed her neck, a brief touch of his lips that left her needing more. So much more.

She wouldn't turn around. She couldn't.

'You're talking in riddles and I don't like it,' she said, her unruly hormones battling with her common sense, urging her to take advantage of the moment while her voice of reason screamed at her to run.

He didn't answer, trailing delicate, soft kisses up her neck to her earlobe as her heart thumped faster. *Oh…my…God…stop…don't stop…* She couldn't think straight. The touch of his hot mouth was sending her wavering resistance flying overboard.

Time ceased to exist as he pressed against her, rocking ever so gently in time with the shifting deck beneath them. Her body burned, needing to feel his bare skin against hers, aching for him to assuage the deep-seated yearning he'd started within her.

They swayed together for what seemed like an eternity, hands interlocked and his groin spooning her, though he didn't push her and his patience shattered any lingering doubts. Why couldn't she live for the moment? She'd never done anything as wildly romantic as this, sailing on a yacht with a drop-dead gorgeous man who didn't hide the fact that he wanted her. What harm could it do?

Slowly disengaging, he turned her around, his gaze never leaving hers. 'I have a solution to all your problems.'

'I just bet you do.' Amber stared, transfixed, drowning in the endless depths of his eyes, which had darkened to almost black. She inhaled sharply, his masculine smell combining with the tang of salt air and sending her already precarious senses spiralling dangerously out of control. She wanted him with a ferocity that scared her, had a burning desire to be caressed by him for endless hours.

Just as she reached for him her common sense kicked in. What was she doing, about to make out with a guy on a boat in broad daylight, in full view of anyone who happened to sail by?

She pulled away, her brain telling her she was doing the sensible thing while her body screamed for more. Resisting the urge to wrap her arms around him, she shrugged out of his embrace and walked to the other side of the boat, putting as much physical distance between them as possible. Right now, her will-power was at an all-time low.

'You were saying?' She steadied her breathing and aimed for nonchalance, hoping he would go along with it.

He stared at her, his passion-glazed eyes doing little to calm her rampaging hormones. 'I can't remember. I sort of got sidetracked.'

'Your solution to my problem?' She drank her fill as he lifted a hand and ran it through his hair, giving her a tantalising glimpse of tanned, washboard abs. For a lawyer who probably spent his days behind a desk he had the body of an athlete, a well-toned athlete in his prime. Her fingers itched to slide down the lean, smooth hardness of his stomach. And lower.

'Oh, that.' He grinned, a devilish glint in his eyes. 'It's simple, really. Marry me.'

CHAPTER FOUR

DESPITE the warmth of the sun as it burst out from behind the clouds, a sudden chill flooded Amber's body.

'What did you just say?'

'You heard me. Marry me.'

She took a steadying breath, hoping he had a logical explanation for his ludicrous suggestion. 'You brought me all the way out here to ask me *that*? I thought you had a serious solution to my family's problems.'

'I'm deadly serious.' He thrust his hands in his pockets, his low, steady voice and confident posture only serving to rile her further.

'You're crazy. Is this some warped, rich-boy's game? Offer marriage in exchange for a roll in the sack? Because if it is, don't worry about it.' Her voice had risen several octaves and she calmed it with effort. What was it about this guy that had her so mad she could shove him overboard without a qualm? 'I don't need a wedding band to have sex with someone.'

She hadn't thought Steve was the type of guy who needed to make empty promises in exchange for

sexual favours; heck, she'd practically offered herself to him on a plate. So why mention marriage?

His features tightened. 'Aren't you taking the
hippy act a tad far? Into free love, are you?'

Heat flooded her cheeks as his barb hit home. 'I'm
not into anything where you're concerned.'

His eyes narrowed and he folded his arms, leaning
back against the railing as if he had all the time in
the world to convince her otherwise. 'Could've
fooled me.'

'Take me home. Now.' She drew herself up to
her less than impressive height of five-six and
glared, furious that he was right. If there were a
vaccination available against tall, gorgeous lawyers,
she would be first in line to be immunised.

He shrugged and turned away. 'Whatever you
say. But don't forget that you turned down the best
offer you ever had to save your father's business.'

Oh, he was good. He knew just where to stick the
knife in before twisting it.

Resisting the urge to plant her hands on her hips
and chastise him like a schoolboy, she said, 'How
could *me* marrying *you* save the business?'

'Simple. The carnival would have enough money
to stay open into the next century.' He pronounced
it like a foregone conclusion, with just a glimmer of
victory in his eyes.

Humiliation washed over her at his suggestion,
and at her foolishness for even entertaining the

thought of marriage to this suave lawyer. 'You think I can be bought?'

Her hands clenched into fists, so tight that her nails bit into her palms. She almost welcomed the discomfort; it would take her mind off the other pain in the vicinity of her heart. She couldn't believe she'd been stupid enough to start liking this guy after one day. All it took was dinner, a boat-ride, a few kisses and she was anyone's. Pathetic.

'I'm not buying you. Think of it as a merger between two interested parties.' By the sombre expression on his face, he seemed to welcome the ludicrous idea as much as she did. So why suggest it in the first place?

'Are you out of your mind?' Her voice had risen to a shriek and she calmed it with effort. 'Marriage should be about love, respect and growing old together, not some sick business notion. I wouldn't marry you if you were the last man on this planet.'

OK, maybe she believed in a fairy tale that didn't exist, but if and when she gave up her freedom for a man it would be for a 'till death us do part' kind of love.

'Even if it means saving your father's dream?'

Wham! He drove that knife in just a little further. She paused for a moment, letting his words sink in. Could she consider this outrageous scenario in order to repay her father for the years of unwavering love and support?

Guilt lent a helping hand to Steve's knife, embedding it deeper; if she hadn't gone to university maybe the business wouldn't be in this position today? Rather than helping her father, she'd followed her dream to gain a business degree in the hope of one day opening her own aromatherapy shop. She'd put her own selfish dream ahead of her dad's and she owed him. Big-time.

'What do you get out of this farcical marriage? Or are you just doing this out of the kindness of your heart? You know—the wealthy prince taking pity on the down-and-out waif.' She couldn't believe she was even considering his proposal, and the rising bitterness was evident in her words.

He blew out a breath in a heavy huff, as if stating the obvious. 'I like you. We'd be a good team. I need a wife; you need a saviour for your family business. It makes sense.'

He made it sound so logical, so normal, when in fact she thought he'd lost his mind.

'Let me get this straight. *You* need a wife and think *I* fit the bill?' Her laughter bordered on hysterical. 'I can see why you might think that. After all, we've got so much in common. You like fast cars; I like slow bushwalks. You like owning a yacht; I like sharing the ocean. You make money for a living; I make people of all ages happy by bringing a little carnival magic into their lives.' She tapped her temple as if pondering over a puzzle. 'Yeah, I can see we're more than compatible.'

He ignored her sarcasm and moved in for the kill,

hitting her where she was most vulnerable. 'What about our attraction?' His low, husky voice rekindled the memory of his kisses, his hands, and the desire that flowed between them, always simmering beneath the surface.

'What attraction?' She couldn't look him in the eye, wishing she hadn't responded to him so eagerly. Her body didn't lie and he'd read all the signals; unfortunately, he was using it against her now.

He covered the short distance between them and held her chin, tilting her head up. 'I thought you said truth was all-important.'

She couldn't deny him. 'It is. So what if there's a few sparks between us? Doesn't mean a thing.'

'You're wrong.' He spoke so softly she barely heard him. 'Mutual desire is a solid foundation for a marriage. Most unions I know started with less.'

She couldn't tear her gaze away, he held her mesmerised with just a look. 'Not where I come from. Haven't you heard of that essential ingredient, love?'

The sardonic twist of his lips made her wonder who had done a job on this guy. Maybe some woman had loved and left him? Interesting, considering that meant he might actually have a heart.

'It's overrated. Why not settle for respect, friendship and a sizzling sex-life?'

Oh, no. She wouldn't waver, despite the erotic images that filtered through her dazed brain from his logic.

She shook her head. 'I can't, Steve. I need my space, my freedom. Even if it did work for a while, you'd end up hating me in the long run. We're too different.'

He pounced quickly as she wavered, and she had a sudden empathy for his opposition. Fixed beneath that all-seeing grey stare, she felt exposed, brow-beaten and defeated, all at the same time.

'Amber, I like you. From what I've seen, I admire your attitude to life, particularly your loyalty to your father. That's a quality I'd value in anyone, especially a wife.' His thumb wandered from her chin to her cheek, stroking with a tenderness that surprised her. 'I know this union will be mutually satisfying.'

She ignored the raging butterflies in her stomach as he continued to caress her cheek. He'd effectively wiped out all her arguments and she couldn't think of anything else to say. Except yes.

Though she'd be damned if she gave in that easily.

'Let me think about it,' she said, already knowing her life-changing answer and wishing her options weren't so limited.

'That's all I ask.' He dropped a chaste kiss on her cheek, causing acute disappointment to filter through her disorientated senses. 'Though I'll expect an answer by the time I get back from Sydney in a day or two.'

She'd been kissed, fondled and propositioned all in the short space of the last hour and he expected her to think straight? She would keep him guessing.

'Fine. Can we head back now?' She needed to escape the confines of the boat and the overwhelming presence of this man who had just turned her life upside-down.

'No rest for the wicked, huh?' His gaze skimmed her body, leaving her in little doubt as to why he'd labelled her as such.

'For your information, I have a massage class to attend.'

'This just gets better and better.' His smile widened as he focused on her hands. By the licentious expression spreading across his face, she could guess what he imagined her hands massaging.

'Wipe that grin off your face. I don't need anyone to practise on. I'm quite competent as it is.' Though the thought of running her hands over his bare skin, stroking the hard lines and sinews of his body, was far from abhorrent. In fact, it left her downright breathless.

'Oh, I'm sure you are. Yet another invaluable skill I value in a spouse.' He turned away, missing her killer look.

Amber didn't speak on the return journey, lost deep in thought. Thankfully, Steve respected her silence and concentrated on handling the boat.

She could get used to this. She'd never had the experience of being pampered; she barely had enough money to buy her treasured crystals these days. Yet here she was, cruising with a man who set her world on fire, contemplating being joined to him in holy matrimony.

Things could be worse. And she could save her dad in the process. She would accept Steve's proposal in a few days and make the most of it. After all, hadn't she done that her entire life? The energy surrounding them felt right, and she'd always trusted her intuition in the past. Why would it fail her now?

However, despite her positive spin on the situation, one thought niggled. Children. She loved them, and had planned on having three or four little ones, yet she would never bring a child into a loveless marriage. Ever. She wanted to emulate her parents' feat, raising her with all the love and support they could give her.

Yet that would never happen now—unless she was foolish enough to fall in love with her husband when he'd clearly stated this would be a business arrangement, a marriage of convenience.

No, she wouldn't put herself through that. She might be willing to sacrifice part of her life to assuage her guilt, yet she wasn't a sadist. She'd take what she could from their union, put on a happy face and avoid the subject of children altogether. If he questioned her, she'd fob him off. End of story.

Studying the man about to become her husband from beneath her lashes, she acknowledged one thing: practising the art of procreation was going to be a lot of fun.

* * *

Steve strode into the office of Byrne and Associates, eager to present his plan. He'd come straight from the airport, barely stopping for a brief shower and change of clothes at his apartment. What he had to say to his fellow partner and founder of the firm, Jeff Byrne, couldn't wait.

As he greeted the receptionist, Matt Byrne approached.

'Hey, Rockwell. How did it go up on the Gold Coast?'

They shook hands, and Steve schooled his face into a mask of indifference.

'Not bad, though there's some unfinished business up there. In fact, that's what I want to talk to Jeff about.'

Matt smiled. 'Whatever you have to say, it shouldn't be a problem. Dad just found out he's about to be a grandfather.'

'That's great. Congratulations.' He slapped Matt on the back. 'You and Kara certainly didn't waste any time, did you?'

'Yeah, well, she's a wonderful woman.'

'I know.' Steve's relationship with Kara had ended a long time ago, and he didn't begrudge Matt his beautiful wife. They had never quite gelled; in fact, Steve had treated her downright badly—a fact she occasionally teased him about these days. 'Listen, could I run something by you?'

Matt cast him a quizzical look. 'Sure. What's up?'

Steve ushered Matt into his office and closed the door. 'I've got this plan, and I have a feeling you're about to become a major player in it.'

Matt sat down, clasped his hands behind his head and leaned back. 'Spit it out, man. I'm hooked.'

Steve took a deep breath, hoping he wasn't making the biggest mistake of his life. 'I want to expand the firm up north and open an office in Brisbane. That would leave a position for a partner free here...' He trailed off, knowing that Matt wanted a partnership in the firm more than anything. Hell, the guy had almost decked him over a year ago when Steve had got the position ahead of him.

'Sounds great, though I thought you didn't like Queensland? What's the catch?'

'No catch. I just need a change of scenery, and the place isn't that bad once you get to spend a bit of time there. You know how it is.' He shrugged, trying to maintain a cool front.

Matt's perception hadn't dulled one iota; that was what made him a top lawyer and Steve respected him for it. 'No, I don't know how it is. Why don't you tell me?'

Steve planned on keeping his explanations about Amber brief. 'I met someone.'

Matt dropped his hands, rubbed them together and leaned forward. 'I knew it. The great man has fallen. She must be incredible to have snared you in a couple of days. What's she like?'

Amber's image rose before Steve's eyes and his

reaction was instantaneous; he'd never been this aroused, even as an adolescent. She'd better say yes to his proposal, otherwise he'd be forced to take action anyway—like kidnap her to a remote Whitsunday island for a long, leisurely seduction.

'She's a stunner. Smart, witty, intelligent, with a rapier tongue.' However, it wasn't words that thoughts of her tongue conjured up. No, he'd experienced its other talents first-hand, leaving him with a distinct hankering for more.

Matt chuckled. 'Well, well, well. The man has finally met his match. Can't wait to meet this miracle woman. Though she can't be all that smart if she's willing to take on the likes of you.'

Steve grinned. 'You'll meet her soon enough. After all, she's going to be my wife.'

'What?'

'Long story. I'll tell you all about it some other time.'

Like never. The Rockwells never aired their dirty laundry; no, they buried their family secrets beneath layers of hypocrisy and platitudes. He hoped he never had to tell Amber the truth behind his proposal, for she would never forgive him. Marrying for money was one thing; producing an heir to secure the fortune of a dying woman would be inexcusable, especially after she'd spouted all that stuff about love.

No, he could never tell her. He just hoped she'd

grow to like him enough to want his child. Thankfully, the private investigator he'd hired to check into the Lawrences' background had provided him with the vital information he needed: Amber was a healthy twenty-three-year-old female who should have little trouble conceiving.

His heart clenched with some strange, indefinable emotion when he thought about Amber with her belly swollen with his child. He knew he'd be a good father; hell, he'd take those new-age parenting classes if needed, and provide his child with so much more than he'd been given growing up.

Matt shook his head. 'I hope you know what you're doing. Not that I'm raining on your parade, or anything, but isn't all this a bit sudden? And what about the deal for Water World?'

Steve had been battling his demons of doubt all night and on the flight down this morning. He didn't need Matt voicing his thoughts all over again.

'She's worth it, Byrne.' Suddenly, he knew he meant it, and it scared him more than anything. 'And someone else will have to represent Water World, seeing as I've switched sides now.'

'Oh, well, don't say I didn't warn you.' Matt thrust out his hand. 'Good luck, my friend. It happens to the best of us.'

Steve shook it. 'Thanks. Give my congratulations to Kara. And don't forget to invite me to the christening.'

'Hey, I'm counting on it. After all, I can't wait to meet—what's her name, by the way?'

'Amber.'

'Mmm. Pretty.' Matt waved as he opened the door.

'Yes, she is.' Reinvigorated with a clear purpose, Steve walked down the corridor and knocked on Jeff Byrne's door. The sooner he cleared up the necessities down here and got back to the Gold Coast, the better.

Forty-eight hours had passed since Amber had last laid eyes on Steve and every one of them had dragged. How could she be this smitten by some arrogant jerk who had proposed to her after knowing her for only two days?

Easily. He'd got under her skin and now she could think of little else. Even the tarot cards she consulted for occasional confirmation of her life choices had turned into the enemy, reinforcing that her marriage to Steve Rockwell was the right path to take.

Rubbish! She should have listened to her high-school friends and torn them up when she had the chance. Though she'd been pretty accurate with her predictions of twins for Laura, a year-long overseas sojourn for Michaela and a famous-actor husband for Meg. Oh, well, they were probably worn out by now. Time to try something new, like runes.

A knock at the door brought her back to the present. 'Come in.' Her heart thudded in anticipation, wondering if the man she'd just been daydreaming about had returned.

'What's my favourite daughter doing hiding in here?' Colin Lawrence stuck his head around the caravan door, a smile creasing his face.

'Hi, Dad. Just doing a bit of meditation. Why don't you join me?'

Her father laughed. 'You know I'm not into all that weird stuff. Next you'll be suggesting I need to sit under a pyramid or something.'

She joined in his laughter. 'Don't knock it till you've tried it.' She paused for a moment, wondering how she could broach the subject of her pending nuptials. Now was as good a time as any to tell her dad; either way, he would think she'd gone nuts.

She scuttled over to make room for him on the tiny sofa. 'Dad, I need to discuss something with you.'

He searched her face, as if looking for clues. 'What's up, love? Haven't seen you this serious in a while. Has that lawyer been bothering you again?'

She shook her head. 'No, but it has got something to do with him.'

She wiped her damp palms against her shorts, hoping for divine intervention at this point. However, none came, and she knew the best way to deliver her news was quickly and straight to the point. 'Dad, Steve proposed to me a couple of days ago.'

Her father almost leapt off the sofa. *'He what?'*

She laid a calming hand on his forearm. 'I know this is hard for you to understand, but we hit it off. I've never felt like this about a man before.' She had that right! 'I think he'll make a good husband.'

She could have sworn her father aged ten years before her eyes. He just sat there, shaking his head from side to side, with his mouth gaping open.

She continued, giving him time to compose himself and before she lost any of her momentum. 'It's a quick decision, but it's for the best.'

Finally, her dad spoke. 'Honey, you're making a big mistake. I've let you live your own life, and supported you where possible, but aren't you taking this free-spirit attitude a bit far? For heaven's sake, you hardly know this man.' Her dad wasn't prone to theatrics, so his fist thumping into his opposite hand shook her more than she let on.

She'd known this would be difficult but there was no way she could back down now. She owed her dad, though she could never tell him the truth behind her marriage. 'You hadn't known Mum long before you married.'

'That was different.' Her father shrank back, his shoulders sagging, and she wondered if he'd ever get over his grief at losing Summer Lawrence.

A pang of sorrow pierced her heart. 'I'm just like her, Dad. Mum instilled her love of life, her live-for-the-moment attitude in me. I've followed in her footsteps so far and it hasn't steered me wrong.' A lone tear trickled down her cheek and she dabbed it away. 'I can't change who I am. Marrying Steve Rockwell is what I want to do. It's the *right* thing to do.'

Her father opened his arms and she leaned into them. 'Having you by my side has been a godsend, love. Ever since I lost your mother you've been my reason for living.' He stroked her hair, just as he had when she'd been a child. 'I've trusted your judgement and you've never let me down. Are you sure this is what you want?'

She pulled away slowly and nodded. 'Yes, Dad.'

'Has this got anything to do with the business?' Her father's shrewdness had always been a problem; he'd grilled every potential date when she was a teenager and hadn't changed when she'd grown up. She'd known he might put two and two together and come up with four.

'No, it hasn't. Though Steve did mention that money wouldn't be a problem once we married and I could use it any way I see fit.' Well, he hadn't used those words exactly, but she'd got the general gist of his businesslike proposal.

A glimmer of hope sprang into her father's eyes. 'Do you think that's true?'

She patted his hand and breathed a sigh of relief. All the fight had gone out of her dad. Now all she had to do was tell the man in question she'd agreed to his proposition and prepare for a life-change that still had her head spinning. 'Everything will be fine, Dad. You'll see.'

Amber wished she felt as confident as she sounded.

As the plane touched down at Coolangatta Airport, Steve reached for his briefcase. He didn't have time to waste. All his carefully arranged plans hinged on an answer from the woman who had him champing at the bit. And it had better be the correct answer, otherwise God help them both.

He didn't bother hiring a car this time. If Amber said yes, he'd whisk her away in the limo and back to his hotel before she had a chance to change her mind. And there was more than one advantage to that little scenario: having her ensconced in his bed would prevent her from running away and have the added bonus of easing the terrible ache which hadn't subsided since he'd met her.

Amber had to say yes. She just had to. Time was running out for his grandmother and he wanted to present his new wife to her as soon as possible. When he'd spoken to his grandma last night her frailty had shocked him. He'd promised to visit in the next week, hopefully with his wife in tow.

As *Col's Carnival* came into sight Steve rummaged through the necessary paperwork he'd brought along for a marriage licence. Once again, he'd gone behind Amber's back and obtained the required documents so that they could marry as soon as possible; for once, he'd been grateful for the power his family name held and the influence that extended even further than he'd thought possible.

Confident that everything was in order, he snapped the briefcase and its precious contents shut as the limo slid to a halt.

'Wait for me, Sam. I won't be long.'

The polite chauffeur tipped his hat in acknowledgement as Steve strode through the gates and turned in the direction of Amber's van.

He'd been shocked when he'd first discovered she lived in a caravan, but had hidden it well. Not everyone had the privilege—or, as he liked to see it at times, the burden of endless family wealth. Besides, the quaint van with its hand-painted mural of dolphins swimming in the ocean fitted the image of the spirited woman who had managed to sneak beneath his guard.

He knocked twice, running a finger beneath the collar of his shirt and suddenly wishing that he'd worn something more comfortable. The humid Gold Coast climate wasn't conducive to suits, though he'd be damned if he ever dressed like some of the locals, who favoured shorts above all else, even for business.

The door was flung open and his heart picked up tempo at the sight that greeted him.

'Hey, there, hotshot. How was the trip?' Amber stood in the doorway, wearing a pair of skimpy cutoff denim shorts and a tie-dye top that bared her midriff. He'd been right. She sported a navel-ring with a glittering purple stone that beckoned like a beacon. Predictably she was barefoot, the silver toe-ring catching the sunlight. He'd never seen a woman so tempting in all his life.

He thrust his hands into his pockets before he reached towards her and did something really stupid, like pull her into his arms and kiss her senseless.

'The trip was fine. I believe you have something for me?'

Confusion flittered across her face and she stared at him with those hazel eyes he could drown in, their unique colour reminding him of a watering hole he'd once seen in the Outback, whose spectacular beauty had stayed etched on his memory. No other colour had come close to emulating what he'd seen at sunrise on that dusty morning years ago. Till now.

'I'm not sure I know what you mean.' She scuffed one bare foot over the other, reminding him of a recalcitrant schoolchild.

'I want your answer, Amber. And it had better be the correct one.'

Her response wasn't quite what he'd expected. She stepped back and slammed the door in his face.

CHAPTER FIVE

AMBER took a steadying breath. She couldn't believe she'd just done that. A loud knock, more insistent this time, had her reassessing the wisdom of her impulsive action.

She wrenched the door open and feigned a casualness she didn't feel. 'Oh. You're still here.'

'What the hell was that all about?'

If he took one step towards her she'd slam the door again, and bolt it this time. He looked mad as hell.

She shrugged, wondering why she enjoyed baiting him so much. 'I just didn't like your attitude, that's all.'

'I asked a simple question, Amber. And you owe me an answer. Nothing more, nothing less.' Though he spoke quietly, she noted the crossed arms, the rigid stance. She had him on the back foot and he didn't like it, not one little bit.

'What if I said that I'm still thinking about your offer?' She bit back a grin as his fists clenched. *Oh, yeah*, she had him exactly where she wanted him.

'I'd say you're a fool. Time has run out.' He stepped up into the doorway and she had to back up, conceding ground.

She planted her hands on her hips and smiled. 'Now, is that any way to talk to your *future wife*?'

He recovered quickly, she'd give him that much. He stood stock-still for less than five seconds, then her words galvanised him into action. He pushed his way into the van and kicked the door closed with a deft flick of his foot. Her confidence drained away as he reached towards her.

'Clever girl,' he said, pulling her flush against his body and running his hands over her bottom.

'Oh, yeah, I'm a regular Einstein.' She gasped as he pressed against her hips, sending desire spiralling through her overheated body. She'd never been greeted like this before and her insides quivered. She was wildly exhilarated yet slightly terrified at her response to the man she would soon marry.

With one hand holding her against him, the other cradled her cheek as he stared into her eyes. 'Shut up and kiss me.'

And she did, standing on tiptoe to wind her arms around his neck and pull his head down, not stopping till his lips melded onto hers in a fiery reaction.

His kiss reminded her of how much she'd missed him, how much she'd yearned for his touch. She'd never hungered for physical release before, thinking sex was a highly overrated exercise. However, as he nibbled and nipped at her bottom lip, and his tongue flickered and teased, she knew that this foreplay would lead to a mind-blowing experience she'd only dreamed about.

She had an irresistible urge to explore every inch of his body, the urgency clawing at her tenuous control. Her hands took on a life of their own, stroking his back, exploring unfamiliar territory.

'I'm starving,' he said against the side of her mouth as he trailed a row of tiny kisses upwards, raining them over her eyelids, her nose and her cheek, towards her earlobe.

What was wrong with the man? He could actually think of food at a time like this? She shook her head as his breath tickled the damp skin beneath her ear.

'But not for food.' He licked his way down to her collar-bone while sliding his hands up her ribcage, as if reading her mind.

She braced her hands on his chest as he backed her up against the wall. 'Doesn't this part come after the "I do"?' she panted, her breathing ragged.

He groaned as his hands slid under her top. 'Don't go old-fashioned on me now, sweetheart.'

She almost passed out with the sheer pleasure pulsating through her body as his thumb brushed her breast. She couldn't think straight, let alone answer him, as he kept up the erotic assault on her senses.

The distant tinkle of merry-go-round music wrenched her mind back to the present and she wriggled out of his grasp. Pulling her top down, she tried to summon a glare. 'Don't you think we've got loads to talk about before jumping to the honeymoon bit?'

He stared at her as if she spoke another language.

'There's nothing to discuss. All the details are taken care of.'

'What do you mean?' A spurt of anger at his presumptuousness shot through her brain. How had he known she would say yes?

He looked around the caravan, her home since she'd been ten years old and moved out of her parents' van, with barely concealed distaste on his face. 'All the arrangements are taken care of. We can get married this week. I've reserved a suite for you at my hotel, so let's go.'

Her flame of anger exploded into a fireball of fury. 'Don't you dare tell me what to do! Although I've agreed to become your wife, it doesn't mean I'm some nobody you can order around. I will stay here till we marry, and only leave when I'm good and ready.'

The smile that tugged at the corners of his mouth, the one that had recently driven her wild with wanting him, only served to infuriate her further. 'Lose the tantrums. Otherwise you'll get what's coming to you—and long overdue, if you ask me.'

'And what's that?'

'A spanking.' The hint of a smile turned into a fully fledged grin as he surveyed his hand, his obvious tool of choice to administer her punishment.

'You wouldn't dare!' Her heart thudded as he took a step towards her, his towering presence dwarfing everything in the tiny van.

'Don't tempt me.' He ran a fingertip lightly down

her cheek, quelling her anger with the sudden tenderness in his eyes. 'When do you want to get married?'

She bit back her first retort of 'so I actually get a say in any of this?' She knew he wasn't a man used to asking other people's opinions, and what it must have cost him to consult her over this.

'How about tomorrow?'

His eyebrows shot up. 'You certainly don't waste any time.'

'For my father. The sooner I can help him out, the better.' She felt better saying the words out loud, for she'd be damned if she'd let Steve know the other reason behind her eagerness to wed. Her traitorous body had got her into enough trouble for one day.

He stiffened and stepped away. She missed his touch. 'Fine. How about three o'clock at the hotel gardens?'

'Sounds good to me.' She paused for a moment, suddenly struck by a thought that could threaten their plans and wondering why it hadn't entered her head before now. 'What about the legalities?'

As he leaned back and rested his hands on a cupboard his biceps flexed beneath the cotton of his shirt, and she knew exactly why she'd been distracted from the practicalities. He had a body to die for. And, what was worse, he probably knew it.

'They're taken care of. All you need to do is turn up tomorrow. Leave the rest to me.' He spoke with

precision, and she had a glimpse of the power behind the man. It was something she couldn't define
but it was there, lurking behind the smooth façade,
a hint of controlled authority that wouldn't be
swayed.

She swallowed, trying to ease the dryness of her
throat and wondering what the heck she was doing,
getting involved with a man like Steve Rockwell.

'What about the future?' She kept her voice
steady, though she wanted to rant and rave at the
injustice of placing her trust in a man who could
break her in a second. They hadn't discussed any
important issues, like where they would live and
whether she would still work at the carnival.

'We'll live in Brisbane. I'll be opening a new
branch of the law firm there. Though we need to fly
down to Melbourne shortly, to visit my grandmother.' He said it as a matter of fact, as if she
should have known all along.

'I'm still going to work,' she said, wondering if
he expected her to be the epitome of a rich lawyer's
wife, attending charity events, playing tennis and
'doing lunch'. No way, no how.

Thankfully, he nodded. 'As you wish. I assumed
you'd be helping your father to get this place back
on track.'

'You seem to do a lot of that. Assuming, that is.'
And she wished he wouldn't; it effectively removed
any control she might have.

'It's a part of what I do. And I'm not about to change now.'

By the set of his shoulders and the frown on his face she knew he believed it. Now all she had to do was set about changing his mind.

He straightened and fixed her with a direct stare. 'I'll send the limo for you at two-thirty tomorrow. See you at the altar.'

'I thought it was a bride's prerogative to be fashionably late? Isn't two-thirty a bit early?' She quelled the sudden fear that leapt into her mind. When he'd said 'altar', the dream had become a startling reality. This man was her future husband, for better or worse, for richer or poorer. Those vows should mean something, not signify some empty business arrangement based on attraction. What was she thinking?

'I don't like to be kept waiting.' And with that he opened the door and stepped out into the sunshine, leaving her feeling decidedly sick.

Mrs Steve Rockwell. It had a hollow, false ring to it, and she wondered if he would agree to her keeping her maiden name. By his stance on everything else, she seriously doubted it.

Mum, I hope I'm doing the right thing. She sent a silent plea heavenwards, needing all the reassurance she could get. She often 'spoke' to her mother, finding it strangely comforting, though she knew that even her liberal-minded mother might have had a bit of trouble accepting what her impulsive daughter was about to do.

With a jumble of thoughts swirling through her head, she opened the wardrobe and took out the dress that hung there, wrapped in layers of plastic. When she'd tried it on yesterday a sense of peace had enveloped her, almost as if her mother had stood behind her and hugged her. It had felt right, wearing the dress her mum had worn when she'd married her father all those years ago, and she hoped her marriage would turn out half as well.

Steve's image popped into her mind, the way he'd looked when he'd taken her out on the boat and proposed. Heck, did he know that she was already half in love with him, arrogance be damned?

She hoped not. Her life would be complicated enough without that added burden. Falling in love with Steve? She couldn't. She wouldn't.

But what if she already had?

Steve had never believed in fairy tales. There had been no tooth fairy, no Santa Claus, no loving mother who waited with milk and cookies when he arrived home from school.

He'd grown up with his eyes wide open. No use expecting happy endings because they just didn't happen. And he hated disappointment more than he hated losing. Thankfully, as Amber strolled towards him on the arm of her father, he was far from disappointed. And when she looked at him, that tentative half-smile playing around her mouth, he knew he'd won.

The civil service flew by in a blur of words and promises. All he could remember afterwards was the way Amber had looked, clad in a cream chiffon dress that hung in pointy layers to her ankles, with her hair loosely piled on her head and adorned with fresh flowers. That and the way her hand had felt in his, warm, small, trusting.

He would look after her, that much he'd promised. He took his vows seriously, like everything else in his life, and he knew that the woman with the orphan-Annie expression who had just become his wife needed protection and nurturing, despite what her feisty attitude would have him believe.

Take now, for instance. She paced like a thoroughbred filly at her first race meet, barely pausing long enough to take in the view from the thirtieth-storey penthouse he'd rented. Her hands trailed over the furnishings as if seeking tangible evidence for what she'd done. He downed his champagne in three gulps, still amazed at the hunger raging through his body whenever he glanced at her. And now she was his. It was time to start acting like it.

He picked up a champagne flute and strolled towards her.

'Here. Time to celebrate.'

She turned to him, her eyes wide. He caught a glimpse of fleeting fear before she took the glass from him.

'Thanks.' She dropped her gaze quickly, finding the buttons on his shirt infinitely more interesting than his face.

He reached towards her and caressed her bare arms, unable to keep his hands off her. 'You don't need to be afraid of me.'

She didn't break his hold, though he could have sworn she almost flinched.

'I don't know anything about you.' Her whisper echoed in the silence and his hands stilled, her uncertainty short-circuiting any intention he'd had of rushing her towards the bed and ravishing her body.

'What do you want to know?'

'Anything…everything…' She finally met his gaze, her vulnerability piercing him to the core.

Hell, what had he been thinking? To marry this woman and keep her at arm's length? Of course she'd want to learn more about him, to share his life; he just didn't know if he was ready to do that yet. He'd learned to shield his emotions at an early age. What chance did he have to change now?

Hoping to deflect her, he trailed his hands up her arms to rest them lightly on her shoulders. 'We have all the time in the world.' He stroked the tense muscles under his hands, watching her slowly unravel before him.

'That feels so good,' she murmured, dropping her head forward. The scent of fresh jasmine filled his nostrils, sending an electrical impulse from his smell receptors to his overloaded brain.

'Did I tell you how beautiful you looked today?' he said, wrestling with his libido and wondering how something as simple as a floral wreath could complement her dress. She hadn't worn any jewellery, apart from that infernal toe-ring, which had been clearly visible through the flat sandals she'd worn. As she'd drifted over the lawn towards him he'd thought that she was barefoot, till she'd come closer and he'd glimpsed the single ivory strap over her toes.

Nothing this woman did would surprise him, and arriving barefoot at her own wedding would have confirmed what he already knew; she didn't conform easily and wouldn't be caught dead doing so. He couldn't wait till she met his conservative, immaculately coiffed mother.

'This dress was my mum's.' She swayed towards him as he continued the massage. 'Dad said I looked just like her today.'

'Then your mother must've been a stunner too.'

Her eyes flew open, their gold-flecked clarity driving all rational thought from his mind. 'Speaking of mothers, what are your family going to think of me?'

He'd wondered the same thing himself, though he hadn't lost any sleep over it. The only member of his family that mattered was his grandmother, and he had little doubt that Ethel St John would welcome her new granddaughter with open arms. The old woman loved to do anything that opposed his mother's wishes, and if acknowledging Amber as part of the Rockwells would set his mother on her ear his gran would do it.

He smoothed the frown from Amber's forehead with a finger. 'Don't worry about them. You're married to me, not the family.'

'But won't they have expectations? From what little you've told me, your mother will eat me alive.'

Her persistence touched him. Not only would his mother have a field-day belittling his choice of wife, but she'd enjoy it too.

'Leave her to me. Now, let's forget about them and concentrate on us.' His finger left her forehead and trailed down her cheek. Her lips quivered as he outlined them with his finger; he yearned to slip it inside the warm slickness of her mouth but he held back. She looked ready to bolt.

'Us?' He'd been right. She virtually shook as he drew her into his arms, whether from excitement or trepidation he couldn't tell.

He smiled, hoping to reassure her. 'You. Me. The fact that tonight is our wedding night.'

'Oh, *that*.' She moistened her lips with her tongue, staring at him as she did it. 'Just give me a minute.' He watched awareness flare in her eyes as she slipped from his grasp and padded across the carpet.

She closed the bathroom door, leaving him thoroughly aroused. The little minx was toying with him, no two ways about it. One minute she looked fragile enough to shatter, the next she looked like every man's fantasy with those full lips, lush breasts and bedroom eyes that just begged him to take her.

Shrugging out of his tux, he laid the suit jacket on a chair and loosened his tie, though what he really felt like doing was stripping down to nothing and jumping Amber as soon as she opened the bathroom door. Instead, he settled for setting the mood by turning off the lights and dimming the bedside lamps. No use appearing too eager. He wouldn't want to give his wife the wrong idea; that was, that he could barely function these days for wanting her.

He turned around as he heard the soft click of the latch opening and struggled not to gape. Amber stood in the doorway, framed by a background of light that shone directly through the sheer material draped around her body.

'My God,' he said, knowing this fantasy come to life couldn't be his. He didn't deserve her, didn't want to admit that she scared the living daylights out of him with the power she held over him. He'd never wanted any woman this much and she happened to be his. All his.

'You like?' She flicked off the bathroom light and sashayed across the room, the transparent fabric swishing around her thighs.

He nodded in approval, knowing his words would be totally inadequate. 'You could say that.'

She stopped in front of him and started undoing

his buttons, one at a time. 'Don't you ever lose control?'

His breath hitched as she reached the bottom of the shirt and tugged it free of his trousers, her fingertips skimming the bare skin above his belt. 'Rarely. I like coming out on top.'

He couldn't believe his luck as she undid the belt, slowly. The women he'd bedded in the past had been cool as ice, wanting him to do all the work. He'd never had a woman undress him till now, and he liked it; he liked it a lot. The thought that she might want him as much as he wanted her turned him on, big-time.

'In *all* scenarios?' Her fingertips played around the waistband of his trousers, driving him crazy.

He stilled her hand as it reached for his zip. 'There are times when I like it the other way round. Like now.' He braced his knees against the bed and fell back, pulling her with him.

'Now, this is more like it.' She straddled him, running her hands up and down his torso as she squirmed against his lap. 'Exactly where a woman should be. In total charge of the situation.'

'I've never met anyone like you,' he said, capturing her hands before they drove him to the brink.

'The feeling's mutual…husband.' She bent down and kissed him, playfully nipping at his bottom lip and sucking lightly, an invitation of lips and tongue that urged him to take their sensual game to the next level.

Never one to back down from a challenge, he flipped her onto her back in one fluid motion. There was only so much he could take, and it was time to show his enchanting wife exactly who was boss.

Amber stared up at Steve, marvelling that the sexiest man to walk into her life was now her husband. And, better yet, was about to make passionate love to her.

'Not having second thoughts?' He nuzzled her neck, his wandering lips driving all logic from her brain.

'Not a chance.' She shivered with pleasure as he pushed the strap of her nightie off one shoulder, his mouth covering the skin he bared.

'What is this thing you're almost wearing?' His hands tangled in the folds of the material, scorching her through its thinness.

She sucked in a breath and lifted her hips off the bed as he tugged it downwards in one smooth movement.

'Something designed to entice.' She almost arched off the bed as he shimmied down the length of her body, grasped her foot and started rubbing, knowing any moment his firm, attuned hands would be sliding up her legs, inch by inch.

'Well, it's sure done that, sweetheart, though personally I prefer what's underneath.' His gaze travelled her body, leaving little to the imagination. 'Did you imagine me taking it off you?' His hand slid up her calf with infinite slowness to the back of her knee, one of her ticklish spots.

She giggled and tried to pull away. 'Yes. I wanted you to want me.' She didn't add 'as much as I want you'.

'Well, it worked. Now, let me show you just how much.'

And he did, by brushing lingering kisses across her body, touching her till she burned for him and driving her to the brink of ecstasy and beyond.

'Wow,' she whispered, as he lay beside her, and she reached and removed the foil packet from his hand and tossed it on the carpet. 'You won't be needing this. I'm on the Pill. Health-wise, everything's OK?'

He quelled her momentary doubts with a searing kiss. 'I'd never put you at risk, Amber. You're my wife.'

She smiled, revelling in her newfound power as an erotic woman. 'Then start performing your husbandly duties.'

'Anything you want, sweetheart.'

Amber knew the endearment didn't mean anything, but she lapped it up anyway. With the man of her dreams making love to her, she wanted to capture every minute detail of the moment and relive it at will, like turning the pages of a cherished album to experience the magic again.

Dazed and sated, she stretched beneath him, relishing the slight ache of rarely used muscles. 'I thought that sort of thing only happened in books.'

He shifted his weight off her and cradled her in his arms. 'With us, anything's possible.'

Amber desperately wanted to believe him. She just hoped that he remembered it when the lights came back on.

CHAPTER SIX

AMBER had always been a daydreamer. She would build scenarios in her head, elaborate make-believe scenes that sustained her through the boredom of school and, later, the loneliness once her mum died. One of her favourites involved a rich, handsome husband who whisked her away to live in a mansion and enveloped her with love.

As Steve dropped a brief peck on her cheek and left for the day, she sighed. So much for that particular fantasy.

Her early misgivings had been right; he treated her like a princess in the bedroom, but when the lights came on the shutters descended, effectively blocking her out of his life. She'd expected an open page, where she could read the print; he'd presented her with a closed book. Sure, he treated her well enough, but they acted like polite strangers rather than husband and wife. But what did she expect? For him to fall madly and stupidly in love, as she had?

Despite her good intentions to hold him at arm's length, she'd fallen for him, harder than she could have anticipated. Not that it mattered to him; Steve treated her with cold formality, and she'd learned to respond in similar fashion. And now, to make matters worse, she had to meet his family and pretend that their marriage meant everything to her. How could she pull it off?

At least the carnival flourished, thanks to Steve's generous cash injection. She'd worked closely with her dad, building a solid foundation for the prosperous years ahead, leaving her with time to pursue her dream. Not that she'd mentioned her plans to her husband; she preferred to sort out the nitty-gritty details before presenting him with her business plan. Hopefully, if he saw how much effort she'd put into it, he wouldn't laugh at her.

The phone rang, startling her. Closing the manila folder containing shop-front rentals she'd been perusing, she reached for the receiver. 'Hello, Amber speaking.'

'Don't forget we leave for Melbourne at two. Be ready by midday.' Steve's curt instructions did little to soothe her mood. She'd woken feeling off-colour, probably due to the increasing tension between them. She hated having to curtail her naturally extrovert personality to suit her workaholic husband and taking orders from him did not sit well with her.

'I have plans. You said we'd leave later.'

'Change them.' He muttered a curse and shuffled papers, as if emphasising that he didn't have time for her.

She resisted the temptation to slam the phone down in his ear. 'What if I can't?'

She'd scheduled an appointment with a property developer to look at a new shop in an ideal location. Her dream of operating an aromatherapy shop was so close she could taste it, yet, in typical fashion, what Steve wanted, Steve would get.

An ominous silence stretched between them. 'I haven't got time for this, Amber. Just do it.'

He disconnected before she could reply, leaving her with a distinct urge to throw the cordless phone against the wall.

Instead, she took a steadying breath and did the only thing possible—rang the developer to schedule a shorter meeting.

Steve thrived on pressure. He lapped it up, always striving for bigger and better things. So why didn't the new law firm he'd opened in Brisbane do it for him? He had an array of clients practically breaking down his door for representation, he'd hired the perfect staff and found offices at a reasonable rent, all in less than two weeks. Then why this feeling of restlessness, of wanting to work from home? He'd never done that in his life.

Go on, admit it.

He shook his head, trying to clear the image of Amber, sleep-tousled and sated, from his mind. He hated having to leave home every morning when that was the last sight that greeted him. God, he couldn't get enough of her. She'd cast a spell over him, probably using some of that hocus-pocus stuff she dabbled in. He didn't interfere in her interests and she respected his need for solitude where his business was concerned; the perfect arrangement, just the way he liked it.

Then why did he feel a sense of loss every time he left in the morning? And why did she look at him with those beautiful eyes in such a way that he felt as if he'd hurt her?

He'd told her the truth from the beginning; their marriage was an emotion-free arrangement. So why did he get the feeling she expected more from him, that he'd disappointed her in some way?

The sooner she had a child to lavish attention on, the better. A baby would definitely take the focus off him, and he would secure the one thing that meant the world to him—his grandmother's fortune. He would keep it away from his mother's money-grubbing hands if it was the last thing he did.

Unable to concentrate, he tidied the stack of contracts on his desk and advised Chelsea, the receptionist, that he would be away for the rest of the day. He planned to see his gran, introduce Amber to his mother over afternoon tea and be back in Brisbane by midnight. He couldn't subject her to the inquisition for any longer than that. If Amber survived meeting his mother, he would know she really did possess powers! He stifled a grin, wondering what those ridiculous tarot cards she favoured would say about meeting her mother-in-law, though personally he thought she would be better off not knowing.

Stopping for a caffeine-rich latte, Steve glanced around the riverside café. It was always packed with business people any time of the day. As he scanned the crowd his gaze alighted on a familiar head of sun-streaked blonde hair, bent too closely towards her companion. He stared, seeing but not quite believing the fact that his wife had leaned towards a young man in a pinstriped suit with that gut-wrenching smile she rarely bestowed on him these days. And, to make matters worse, she wore make-up and a sleek, figure-hugging red suit that he'd never seen before.

As her companion returned her smile, Steve wanted to walk over there and beat the man to a pulp. Instead, he took a few sips of his coffee and watched as Amber turned on the charm, laughing, flirting, appearing interested in the papers the other guy offered her. So these were 'the plans' she'd told him about over the phone. And he'd been stupid enough to think that all her plans revolved around her father, the carnival and him.

He drained the last of his coffee and almost slammed the empty glass on the counter. No one played him for a fool, particularly not the woman he'd chosen for his wife. OK, so maybe she'd conned him with her innocent routine but when it came right down to it she was no different from his mother; out for money and everything it could buy.

He knew he'd bought Amber by coercing her into marriage with the promise of money to save the carnival, but a small part of him had hoped she might feel something for him.

Yeah, right. All they had was a marriage of convenience, and the sooner he realised it, the better. As if he needed any further evidence, with the sight of his wife schmoozing up to some cretin in a poorly tailored suit. Yeah, she was just like his mother, using every weapon in her arsenal to get what she wanted. Thankfully, he'd hardened his heart against her; he'd had more than his fair share of let-downs in the past by a woman who was supposed to have loved him; why should Amber be any different?

Casting one last malevolent glare in the direction of his wife, he turned away and stormed out.

Amber couldn't hide her joy. The meeting with the property developer had gone better than expected; once she'd told him about her limited time frame he'd suggested they meet for coffee and look over the plans rather than meet at the actual site. He'd impressed her with his professionalism and she couldn't wait to run her plans by Steve. Thankfully, her husband could handle all the scary legalities while she concentrated on the real business of turning her dream into a reality.

As the front door opened she jumped up from the sofa, a welcoming smile on her face and the familiar thrill of seeing her sexy husband shooting through her. Despite their differences, she couldn't control her fickle hormones or the way they reacted whenever Steve so much as glanced her way.

'Hi. Am I glad to see you.' She needed to share her excitement with someone before she burst.

Steve dropped his briefcase with a loud thud, his icy stare stopping her in her tracks. 'That'd be a first.'

Her smile faltered but she continued; he sometimes returned home from work grouchy, so why should today be any different? 'I'm always glad to see you. We've got loads to talk about.'

'I just bet we have.'

To her amazement, he walked over to the sideboard and poured himself a whisky. The only time she saw him drink was the occasional nightcap, yet now he swallowed the drink in three short gulps, and it wasn't even midday.

'Is everything OK?'

He stared into the empty tumbler before looking up at her, the bleakness in his eyes scaring her more than his drinking. 'You tell me.'

'I—I don't know what you're talking about,' she said, the swift change from bleakness to barely constrained fury chilling her to the bone.

'Yes, you do.' He clenched the glass so tightly, she wouldn't have been surprised if it shattered. 'How about you tell me about your *plans*?'

She sighed in relief, though it was shortlived. If he knew about the proposed shop, his anger could only be directed towards her for not telling him about it. 'Oh, that. I was just about to tell you. How did you find out?'

He laughed, a bitter sound that echoed in the foyer. 'It wasn't that difficult, with you flaunting it for the world to see. What happened to the power suit and the make-up, by the way? Don't you need to dress to impress your *husband*?'

He spat out the last word and she took a step back, suddenly realising what his tirade was about. He'd seen her at the café and, being the typical suspicious male he was, had jumped to conclusions.

Anger flooded her body; he didn't trust her. Heck, he obviously didn't think much of her at all, apart from being a willing and able participant for his bedroom games. Well, he could whistle for it now.

She tilted her head up and glared at him. 'For your information, I needed to present a professional image to the property developer who is helping me locate a site for my business. That's why I dressed up. As for what you're thinking, thanks for the vote of confidence.'

He paled, squared his shoulders and carefully set his glass on the table. 'What business?'

'My own aromatherapy shop. I've done a lot of research into its viability and prepared a business plan for you to check out.' She refrained from adding 'you moron'. His lack of trust hurt more than it should have.

'You want to run a profitable business based on

smelly oils?' He couldn't have looked more sceptical if he tried, sending her blood pressure soaring even higher.

'You would say that,' she snapped, turning away and blinking back the tears that had sprung into her eyes. Not only did he think she'd cheated on him, but he also scoffed at her dream, reducing it to ridicule in less than two seconds. She'd never forgive him.

She heard him walk across the polished floorboards towards her.

'Let's talk about this.' He placed a hand on her shoulder and tried to turn her around.

'Leave me alone.' She shrugged off his hand and ran towards the stairs, not wanting to give him the satisfaction of seeing her cry.

Thankfully, he didn't come after her, though a small part of her wished he would apologise, sweep her into his arms and kiss and make up.

Instead, he issued a command in his usual inimitable style. 'Don't forget we leave in fifteen minutes for the airport.'

She resisted the urge to flip him a rude sign, and continued up the stairs to the safety of their room, tears trickling down her face.

Steve watched her go, feeling like the biggest bastard in the world. So much for his years of training; he'd handled that with the finesse of a squatter at a landlord's convention, all loud demands and not much listening.

Hell, he'd hurt her. He'd seen the glimmer of tears in her eyes as she rushed past him, and he'd put them there with his accusations. In his defence, what had he been supposed to think when his wife met another man in secret and dressed the part?

You could have trusted her.

Trust wasn't an emotion that sat easily with him. He'd been a gullible child, believing the empty promises of his mother, only to be repeatedly let down when she didn't attend his first soccer game, his first rowing tournament, his first debate. Back then he'd sworn never to trust anybody again, particularly women. Even his grandmother, whom he loved, had her own agenda and didn't fully trust him.

Why else would she stipulate that his child inherit her fortune rather than himself? She'd made a joke of it, saying he had a hard time standing up to his mother and her dream would be better realised if he oversaw the management of her funds rather than handle them himself. What she really meant was that she thought he didn't have the guts to take a stand against his mother, especially when she turned up the heat.

So he'd learned to harden his heart and shut off his emotions, all in the name of self-preservation.

And now he'd hurt the one person who had started to breach his carefully erected barriers, the woman whom he could learn to trust given half a chance.

Stupid, Rockwell. Real stupid. He trudged up the stairs, hoping he could mend the damage he'd inflicted on the one woman who didn't deserve it.

Amber appreciated Steve's apology; she knew how much it must have cost him. However, it didn't change the fact that he thought her dream sucked. Not that he'd said so; she could just tell by his remarks. Rather than embracing her dream wholeheartedly, he'd fired a barrage of technical questions at her, leaving her with a distinct impression that he found her and her business plan lacking.

So much for the support of her spouse. She would just have to do it on her own, like everything else in her life to date.

'We're almost there,' he said, as the taxi drew up outside an imposing set of wrought-iron gates.

Amber craned her neck, trying to get a glimpse of Steve's childhood home. However, the Rockwell mansion, in the exclusive Melbourne suburb of Toorak, was well screened by some of the tallest oaks she'd ever seen. She watched him speak into an intercom and tried to quell her growing apprehension.

All the reassurances in the world couldn't calm her nerves. Steve had said he'd be with her every step of the way but he couldn't change the facts: she didn't belong here, alongside a filthy-rich lawyer, as his wife and, worse yet, pretending that she loved him.

Not that the latter would be difficult. Despite their differences, which seemed to grow with every passing day, and against her better judgement, she'd fallen for him.

'You OK?' He squeezed her hand as he slid back into the taxi after speaking into the intercom.

She nodded, silently thanking him for understanding exactly how she felt.

'We'll see Gran first and leave the best for last.' His serious expression only served to send her nerves into panic mode.

'Is your mum that bad?' She clung to his hand, needing the physical contact to keep her butterflies grounded.

'She's worse,' he said, and grimaced as the butterflies took flight. 'But don't worry. We'll be out of here in a few hours.'

Amber remembered those words as she entered the lavish foyer of the mansion and struggled not to gape. Sure, she'd known the Rockwells were rich, but nothing Steve had told her had prepared her for this: soaring ornate ceilings from which hung several chandeliers, brocade walls covered with oil paintings and a staircase that would have done Scarlett O'Hara proud. Not to mention the marble floor which her heels clacked on.

She performed a slow, three-hundred-and-sixty-degree turn, keeping her jaw firmly clamped. 'What? No servants?'

He shrugged as they entered a large room, which

could only be described as a parlour, filled with overstuffed chairs and priceless antiques. 'Must be Jeeves's day off.'

She stopped short, wondering if he was serious.

He smiled. 'I'm kidding. Come on.'

She trailed after him, carefully picking her way through the maze of bric-à-brac that must have cost a small fortune. This wasn't wealth, it was obscenity. What little spare money she had, she donated to an orphanage in Nepal; the cost of furnishings in this mansion alone could feed and clothe the orphans for the next decade.

Schooling her face into a mask of impassivity, she looked at her husband. 'So this is home?'

His brows drew together, as if he sensed her censure. 'Hasn't been for a long time. Probably never was.'

'Don't you like it?' Curiosity egged her on, as Steve rarely spoke of his family. In fact, what little he'd told her she'd had to drag from him.

He quirked an eyebrow. 'What do you think?'

She glanced around, once again struck by the coldness of the place. It looked like a museum, not a home. 'Not really a place for kids, I suppose.'

'Got it in one. Come on, let's meet Gran.' He tugged on her hand and she gladly followed, eager to escape the imposing room and its tomb-like feel.

He led her through several passages, each lined with mahogany, till they reached the back of the house.

'Through here.' He pushed open a door and she almost gasped at the beauty of the small room. Sunlight flooded through the floor-to-ceiling windows, lending the room an atrium-like feel. Potted plants and vases filled with roses lay artistically arranged on tables, brightening the room further. No clutter of ornaments here; instead, a cream-coloured sofa scattered with gold cushions and a coffee-table covered in copies of upmarket magazines lent a cosy feel while still exuding class. Amber could have curled up with a magazine on the sofa quite comfortably.

'This is nice,' she said, hoping that the aura she sensed in this welcoming room matched the lady who inhabited it.

He smiled, a genuine tilting-up of his lips that softened the hard planes of his face. She hadn't seen him smile like that in a long time and it warmed her heart.

'I love it. When Gran came to live with us she renovated these rooms. They're the only place in this house I ever felt comfortable.'

'I know what you mean. It just has a good feel about it.'

He looked at her and she caught her breath; his smile hadn't dimmed and it did strange things to her insides, especially in the vicinity of her heart.

'You're not doing that mumbo-jumbo stuff again, are you?' His eyes gleamed with amusement.

She tilted her head and sniffed. 'Every place and every person has an aura. It is *not* mumbo-jumbo.'

He held up his hands. 'OK, OK. I was just checking. Don't be so touchy.'

Unfortunately, his words conjured up a vision of him doing just that—touching her with all the skill she'd come to expect from her talented husband. Her thoughts must have reflected in her eyes and she watched awareness spread across his face as he reached for her. Her eyelids fluttered shut as his arms slid around her waist and she waited for the first, scintillating brush of his lips. It seemed like for ever since he'd last kissed her, their disagreement over her clandestine meeting with the property developer having driven a nasty wedge between them, and she longed for his touch.

'Steven, is that you?' The feeble voice came out of nowhere and they sprang apart like two dogs doused with cold water from a hose.

'Yes, Gran. It's me. And I've brought someone to meet you.' He looked down at Amber, the slate of his eyes darkening to ebony as he ran a fingertip down her cheek. 'Later,' he said, in a husky voice laden with promise.

Amber swallowed, trying to calm her pounding heart and steel her nerves for the meeting ahead. She followed him into a bedroom that was almost a mirror image of the lounge room; lined shantung curtains were pulled back to let as much light into the room as possible, and a matching bedspread covered the high four-poster bed, where a frail lady with a shock of white hair sat up and stared at her with eager eyes.

'You must be Amber. Come closer, child. Let me see you.'

Amber stepped forward and held out her hand. 'Pleased to meet you, Mrs St John.'

The old lady gripped her hand with surprising force. 'Likewise, my dear. How is my grandson treating you?'

Amber noticed the shrewd gleam in the old lady's eyes; though her physical appearance seemed fragile, she would bet that nothing escaped her.

'I'm enjoying married life and all its challenges.' Amber couldn't lie; she just hoped the old lady bought her half-truths.

'You didn't answer my question.' As she'd thought, the old lady was on to her in a flash. 'After all, your marriage was rather quick. Is there anything I should know?' She stared at Amber's stomach before casting Steve a pointed look.

Amber glanced from one to the other, totally confused by her husband's quick negative shake of the head and his grandmother's almost conspiratorial wink.

'No. I'm not pregnant. Steve just swept me off my feet.' She hoped her answer would suffice. At least the latter was true; she hadn't stood a chance when this smooth lawyer entered her life and turned it upside-down.

The old lady snorted. 'Well, I'm glad to hear you're happy. Just don't leave the babies too long. I'm not sticking around, remember?'

Steve stepped forward, filling the awkward silence. 'Enough of that talk, Gran. How are you feeling?' He bent and kissed her, his hand dwarfing her gnarled one as he held it.

'As well as can be expected, though this damn cancer knocks me down quicker than one of your mother's barbs.' She grinned, and it lit up her gaunt, wrinkled face, lending it a softer quality in the harsh daylight.

Amber blinked back tears, suddenly transported back to her mother's bedside on that last day. 'Be happy, my darling. Follow your heart, no matter what.' Her mother's last words had stuck with Amber and she'd tried to follow them.

Now, as she stared at her husband, with his head bent close to his grandmother's, she wondered for the hundredth time if she'd done the right thing. She'd followed her heart and married a man she'd fallen for in less than a day in the hope that he might one day love her in return. She just hoped her mum was right; following her heart would be one thing…having it break into a million pieces after years of unrequited love would be unbearable.

Steve stood up and reached for her hand. 'We must go. Gran is tired.'

The old lady smiled up at her. 'You're a vision,

my dear. Steven is lucky to have found someone like you. Take good care of him.'

Impulsively, Amber bent down and kissed the papery cheek. 'It's been a pleasure to meet you. Take care.' She knew her words sounded inadequate but she meant them from the heart.

By the look on her face the old lady truly loved her grandson, a trait they shared.

Steve squeezed her hand, and Amber knew she'd passed the first test. If only meeting her dreaded mother-in-law could be this easy.

He patted his grandmother's hand. 'I'll be down in Melbourne next week. See you then.'

The old lady waved at them, a sheen of tears glazing her eyes as they left the bedroom and closed the door.

'She's incredible,' Amber said in a whisper, relishing the feel of her husband's hand gripping hers. They rarely touched outside the bedroom, a fact she would like to change, given half a chance.

She knew Steve's coolness hid a wealth of fiery passion, a warmth just dying to burst free if only he would let it. However, after seeing this house, she had some idea of why he suppressed his feelings. How could anyone live in a mausoleum like this and express any normal emotion? He just didn't know how. Luckily, she was a good teacher.

'She's amazing, all right. I just wish there was something I could do, dammit.' His brow furrowed and she yearned to reach up and smooth it.

Her heart ached with empathy. 'Just be there for her. And if she has any last requests, do your best. That's what she would want.'

Steve looked away and she wondered about his sudden evasiveness. He'd been acting strangely since they had entered his grandmother's bedroom, but then who could blame him? He had to sit back and watch the only woman he loved dying before his eyes. If anyone could understand what that did to a person, she could.

'I'm trying. Believe me, I'm trying.' He looked as if he wanted to say more but seemed to bite back the words.

She wondered if it had been the mention of children that had him on edge; she'd noticed the assumed blankness that descended when his grandmother had mentioned it, followed by that vehement negative nod. They still hadn't spoken about it. What would he think of her secret cravings for a brood of youngsters to fill her life with love and laughter? And, more importantly, her need for a normal, love-filled marriage before she would even consider bringing a child into this world?

From the impenetrable look on his face as he squared his shoulders for the upcoming meeting with his mother, she had a fair idea. Their marriage was business, as he reminded her on a daily basis. He didn't have room in his well-ordered life to love anyone and she'd be well served to remember it.

'Ready to meet Mother?'

Amber nodded. So what if she felt as if she was about to face a firing squad? She'd done worse…like walk down the aisle and marry a man whom she hardly knew. And then expect him to love her.

Compared to that, meeting the infamous Mrs Rockwell would be easy.

CHAPTER SEVEN

AMBER closed her eyes and leaned back as the plane taxied down the runway and took off. 'Drained' would only begin to describe how she felt after afternoon tea with Georgia Rockwell; try pummelled, browbeaten, interrogated and thoroughly chewed up and spat out.

Yeah, that was more like it. From the first minute the designer-clad woman had laid eyes on her she'd turned up her pert nose and kept it there, treating her new daughter-in-law like an unwanted disease.

Sure, she'd appeared polished and refined, from the top of her French chignon to the soles of her imported stilettos, but her calculated barbs had struck home on several occasions, leaving Amber feeling like a voodoo doll stabbed by a million pins. If she'd thought Steve had some hang-ups, she'd done him a disservice. She should give him a medal for turning out as well as he had, considering his mother.

'Do you want something to eat?' Steve's solicitous tone only served to rile her further. She wanted to rant and rave against the injustice of having had to face that woman; it was all his fault.

Her eyes flew open and she fixed him with a

glare, blaming her rolling stomach on unresolved tension rather than lack of food. 'I'm not hungry.'

'How about a drink, then? Looks like you need one.'

If he smiled, she would hit him. 'No thanks to you.'

'Hey. What did I do?' He tried to look innocent and failed miserably. Besides, with that striking face, and eyes that could pierce her to her soul, she seriously doubted Steve Rockwell had ever looked innocent in his entire life.

'You could have warned me.' A little voice inside her head reminded her he had—but nothing could have prepared her for the harridan that passed as Steve's mother.

The smile that had been threatening to drive her over the edge suddenly broke through. 'I did. You just didn't listen.'

Despite her anger, her pulse responded in typical staccato fashion. 'She almost ate me alive!'

Amber squirmed at the recollection of her mother-in-law's disgusted look when she'd spied her toe-ring and said, 'What is that *thing*?' Her subconscious, like a devil prodding her with his pitchfork, had tempted her to lift her top and show off her navel-ring too, but she'd succumbed to decorum and ignored it.

'Don't worry about her. I don't.' He accepted two glasses of wine from a stewardess and handed her one. 'Here. This should hit the spot.'

Amber took a sip, enjoying the refreshing crispness of the Barossa grapes she'd quickly grown accustomed to. The wine was just one of the perks of being a Rockwell; she'd rarely flown before, but travelling first class was something she could definitely get used to. Steve had opened her eyes to a world of luxury she'd never dreamed of, let alone thought she could have one day. A pity she couldn't have the one thing she now wanted—his heart.

'We don't really know much about each other, do we?' She noted the sudden tensing of his shoulders, the downward turn of his lips, and for the hundredth time wondered why she couldn't hold her tongue.

'What's there to know?' He turned to face her, the action drawing attention to his broad chest, clearly defined in one of the pale blue business shirts he favoured.

'Well, how you feel about kids, for starters.' There, she'd said it, the true issue that had been niggling since this afternoon. If she was completely honest with herself she'd been wondering about it since she'd first agreed to his hare-brained scheme of her becoming his wife.

He drained the remainder of his wine before speaking. 'I want a child.' He spoke with all the conviction of a man sentenced to hanging. In fact, with his voice so devoid of emotion, he sounded as if he would rather choose a noose than a bassinet and nappies.

'Try to curb your enthusiasm.' She picked up the

in-flight magazine and flicked the pages, not really seeing anything beyond a few pictures, trying to control her growing disappointment. What had she expected? For the man who preferred his office to his home to suddenly jump over the moon about fathering a child?

He reached over and plucked the magazine from her fiddling hands. 'Look, don't go getting all emotional on me. You knew the score when we married. Sure, I want a child. In fact, the sooner the better.'

Amber gaped. 'Why?'

Once again, he didn't meet her eyes. 'Isn't that what you want?'

'How did you know? And since when did what I want come first?' She didn't understand his turnaround. In fact, she didn't understand anything about the enigmatic man she'd married, period.

'I saw the way you acted around the kids at the carnival. Not to mention the hope on your face when Gran looked at your stomach and hinted at the possibility of pregnancy. You want a child, and I'm not going to stand in your way.'

She quelled her sudden flare of hope. 'Having a child is a huge step. I won't bring a defenceless baby into this world unless both parents are willing to give it all the love and support it deserves.'

'And you think I can't do that?' He crossed his arms, his anger evident in his rigid neck muscles.

A vision of the Rockwell mansion and its matriarch in all their icy splendour flashed into her mind and she wondered if this man who had grown up there was capable of any emotion remotely resembling love. 'Money can't buy love, Steve.'

'Oh, no?' His gaze skimmed her body, as if reinforcing the fact that he'd certainly paid a price to obtain her.

Fury surged through her and she took a steadying breath before she did something stupid, like slam his meal tray into his lap and permanently damage any chance he might have of fathering offspring. 'So, did you get value for money on *this* deal?'

'Don't cheapen what we have, Amber.'

Her anger must have tainted her sight, for she could have sworn she saw a flicker of hurt in his eyes. 'I didn't do that. You did, the minute you offered to bail out my father's business in exchange for a bride.'

His eyes narrowed to an electrifying grey. 'And your complaint is…?'

She wanted to scream, to smash open the tiny window and jump out of the plane, parachute be damned. 'You don't get it, do you? I don't like being controlled. I don't like being told what to do. And I especially don't like you sitting there like some paragon of virtue pretending you want to bring children into this farce of a marriage.'

He stared at her as if she'd grown two heads. 'Are you finished?'

How did he do it? That ultra-cool façade, the thinned lips, the smirk, the slight tilt of an eyebrow.

Arrogant jerk…and she was stupid enough to have fallen in love with him.

She didn't respond. Instead, she turned away and stared out of the window, hoping he would leave her alone.

'This isn't finished, sweetheart. Not by a long shot.'

She frowned and tried to ignore the waft of his intoxicating signature aftershave as he leaned towards her.

His voice dropped seductively low. 'Who knows? You might even want to practise making babies when we get home?'

Despite her best intentions, her stiff posture softened at the thought of them in bed together. A slow-burning heat flooded her body at the memory of his hands, his tongue and his consummate skill at wielding them. He didn't touch her; he didn't have to. She would have joined the mile-high club in an instant if he'd asked her. Thankfully, she mustered every last ounce of resolve and continued to ignore him.

She sensed his capitulation as he settled back in his seat, leaving her to blot out her erotic thoughts. Closing her eyes, she concentrated on meditating, in an effort to centre her psyche. However, for the first time in her life, the image of a man disrupted her deep relaxation.

And, what was worse, she pictured him cradling a child in his arms.

*   *   *

Steve left for the office earlier than usual the next morning, despite the late hour they had arrived home. He needed to get away from Amber so he could think—the one activity he could barely do in her all-invasive presence. She captivated him to the point where he had trouble concentrating on what she said most of the time, with his attention drifting to the remembered delights of her mouth and other equally appealing parts of her anatomy. And, despite their words on the plane, she'd welcomed him with open arms last night as soon as they had entered the bedroom. Well, the shower, to be precise.

God, what a woman. Their marriage of convenience was fast becoming a union of need. He wanted his wife as he'd never wanted any other woman, and it scared him. It scared him to death. He could never let her know the power she held over him otherwise she might use it, just as his mother once had.

As if the mere thought of his mother had conjured her up, the phone rang.

'Yes, Chelsea?' He picked up the phone, knowing it had to be her and wishing otherwise.

'Your mother on line one, Mr Rockwell.'

He rubbed his forehead. 'Put her through, thanks.'

'Steven, darling. So nice of you to pop in yesterday.'

He swallowed a sigh. 'You've been on my case for weeks, Mother, about meeting Amber.'

'Ah, yes...Amber.' She paused, and Steve braced himself for the sure-fire character assassination that would follow. For once, his mother didn't disappoint him. 'She seems to be rather...bohemian.'

'I prefer interesting.'

He heard a polite sniff. 'Oh, I know what you find so *interesting* in that common tramp—'

'Mother, you're talking about my wife.' He snapped the pencil he held in two, a habit he'd picked up when speaking to his mother.

'How could you, Steven? After all the nice young women I've introduced you to? Whatever happened to Brianna?'

He pulled a face, thankful that none of his clients could see him now. His mother always brought out the worst in him and he often resorted to childish behaviour to cope. 'Mother, I haven't got time for this. Is there any particular reason you called, apart from slandering *my wife*?'

This time, the sniff sounded forced. 'I'll be flying to Brisbane next month for a fashion show. Just thought you'd like to know.'

Great. Now he'd be obliged to escort her, he just knew it.

'Of course you'll be accompanying me?' She made it sound like an order, not a question.

'Of course, Mother. Anything else?'

'Your grandmother seems to be a lot perkier since your visit. Perhaps *you* should visit more often?' From her emphasis on 'you', he knew the invitation didn't include Amber, and he could have throttled her for it. How his mother could be the progeny of Ethel St John, he'd never know.

'*We'll* try to get down to Melbourne soon, though Amber's starting up a business and the practice is beginning to thrive up here.' As soon as he said it he knew he should have thought of some other excuse to deflect his mother's invitation. He must be more tired than he thought.

Predictably, she fastened on the fact of Amber's venture. 'Your wife is starting up a *business*?' She made it sound as if his wife planned to become a stripper.

'Yes, in retail. Now, if you don't mind, I really need to get back to work.'

'*Retail?*' He held the phone receiver away from his ear, anticipating the shriek. 'As if you working isn't bad enough, you're encouraging her to be a shop girl? Have you lost your mind?'

For the first time since he'd heard his mother's voice he smiled; imagine if he told her the shop would promote aromatherapy and other alternative products? She'd need a week to recover in some day spa, maybe even a month. Not a bad idea, if it coincided with her proposed trip to Brisbane...

'Steven, are you listening to me?' Her high-pitched octaves had subsided to a dull roar.

'Goodbye, Mother. Speak to you soon.' He hung up without waiting for a response and wondered if he could schedule an emergency conference in Sydney around the time of the fashion show.

Feeling decidedly cheered by the thought, he flipped open the folder of contracts on his desk and started the serious business of representing the best interests of his clients.

Amber threw away her packet of contraceptive pills a few weeks after they returned to Brisbane. Much to her amazement, Steve had changed in ways she'd only dreamed of; he talked about his business with her, he seemed more affectionate outside the bedroom, and most importantly he actively supported her dream of opening *Harmony*. Thanks to his input, the grand opening was scheduled for next week, and funnily enough it coincided with the launch of her other dream, to have a child.

The timing had been perfect, and once he'd urged her to stop taking protection she knew that her life was almost complete. Though he hadn't said it in so many words, she knew he'd grown to care for her, perhaps even love her. Why else would he have changed so much? Why would he ask her to stop taking the Pill unless he wanted a child as much as she did?

As she arranged the crystals on the counter she marvelled at her happiness. How had it happened so quickly? And what had she done to deserve it?

The shop had more than lived up to expectations, stocking everything from oil burners, pure essences and candles to self-help books, jewellery and tie-dyed silk scarves hand-made in Byron Bay. She looked around, amazed at the transformation from empty store to an Aladdin's cave of goodies to tempt any enquiring soul and mind. It was a dream come true, and one man had made it possible.

As if on cue, the back door opened and Steve strolled in, looking every bit the consummate businessman in a killer suit.

'How's my favourite fortune-teller?' He didn't wait for an answer, covering her lips with his in a bruising kiss that took her breath away.

She braced her palms on his chest, revelling in the feel of hard muscle hidden by expensive cotton and cool wool. 'I've already told you. That was only a one-off.'

'Ah, but look where it got you. All that stuff you said about me when we first met just stoked my fire and I had to have you.' He leaned into her, lending weight to his words. 'Are you sure you aren't a witch as well?'

She rubbed against him, loving the feel of him. It empowered her to know she aroused him. 'Sorry to disappoint. I travel by car, not broomstick.'

He trailed his hands down her back, cupping her bottom. 'Sweetheart, nothing about you disappoints me.'

'So, what do you think?' She waved in the direction of the stacked shelves surrounding them.

The passion in his eyes as he stared at her did little to calm her racing pulse. 'Incredible.'

Her breath caught as the familiar heat sizzled between them. 'I mean the shop.'

'Oh, that!' He barely glanced around, though she could read the pride in his face. 'Later.'

With one hand holding her close, he reached behind her and pulled a stack of silk-covered cushions off the shelves.

'Hey! No touching the merchandise.' She playfully slapped his arm while snuggling against him.

He quirked an eyebrow before lowering his head and nibbling on her neck in the one spot known to drive her crazy. 'Doesn't this shop have a try-before-you-buy policy?'

'Are you interested in the cushions? They're hand-embroidered in India, you know...' She trailed off as his lips descended to the V of her shirt.

'I'm interested in everything this shop has to offer.' His tongue flickered out, dampening her skin before he blew on it. 'Especially the proprietor.'

Goose bumps peppered her body as he continued to alternately lick and blow on her skin, driving all conscious thought from her brain.

'What if she's not for sale?' She gasped as his fingers slowly undid the buttons of her shirt and, in doing so, brushed against her breasts.

'No problem. I'm into acquiring things that are priceless.' He kissed his way lower and she arched towards him, craving his touch like a madwoman and grateful for the newspaper covering the glass windows.

'The back door...' she murmured, as his hands ran rampant over her body.

'Locked. Relax, sweetheart. Enjoy.'

And she did, startled by the intensity of her husband's lovemaking. She'd never imagined making love on scattered cushions on her shop's floor could be so good, so wild, so unrestrained. She could barely speak when they finally lay spent, entwined in each other's arms.

'I'm proud of you,' he whispered against the side of her mouth as he kissed her.

She snuggled up to him, basking in his praise. Though he never made her feel second-best, Amber felt a strange compulsion to make her husband proud of her. Perhaps it had something to do with their different backgrounds, the fact that she'd always felt as if she had to prove herself worthy of her dynamic husband.

And now she had a secret to tell him which she hoped would seal the emotional validity of their marriage.

'Steve, I have to tell you something.' She stroked the hard sinews of his back muscles, marvelling at the strength beneath her fingertips.

He rarely had time to go to the gym, yet his body stayed firm. She just hoped hers would do the same after nine months on the hormonal rollercoaster that pregnancy entailed, but knew her wish was futile.

Though somehow she looked forward to the changes in her body, knowing they would be testament to the incredible life growing inside her.

His hand curved around her breast. 'Let me guess. The business plan needs revision?'

She drew in a sharp breath as his index finger circled a nipple. 'No.'

He traced lazy circles across her stomach, which would soon be distended with their precious child. 'More stock is needed?'

Her senses reeled as his fingertips edged lower. 'No.'

'You need more of this?' He caressed her, his intimate touch driving all thought from her mind.

'God, yes,' she breathed, giving in to the pleasure of his fingers, his mouth, his body all over again. Her news could wait till later. Much later.

Amber tidied the well-stocked shelves for the final time before unlocking the front door. Taking a deep breath, she flipped the sign to read 'Open' before resuming her position behind the counter. Doubts plagued her mind. What if no one came? What if people scoffed at her merchandise? Would her stock be too New Age? As the bell above the door tinkled she looked up with a tentative smile, eager to greet her first customer.

'Hello, Amber.'

Her heart plummeted, though she fixed a welcoming smile in place. 'How nice to see you again, Mrs

Rockwell.' She resisted the urge to stick her fingers down her throat and make vomiting noises at her falseness. 'What brings you to Brisbane?'

Her mother-in-law pursed her lips in a poor semblance of a smile. 'Didn't Steve tell you we were coming?'

'We?' Amber looked around, wondering if the old battle-axe had dragged along an invisible playmate or was using the royal pronoun in yet another pretentious show.

As if on cue, the door swung open and in walked Cindy Crawford. At least, that was Amber's first thought as a stunning brunette sashayed into the shop as if she owned it.

'This is Brianna. I thought you two should meet, seeing as you have so much in common.' The smirk on her mother-in-law's expertly made-up face made Amber's hand itch.

Resisting the urge to slap her husband's mother and ask what she had in common with this buxom goddess, she gritted her teeth. 'Pleased to meet you, Brianna. If you see anything you like, don't hesitate to ask for help.'

The brunette looked her up and down and Amber could have sworn she saw the supermodel look-alike reel back. '*You're* Steven's wife?'

It didn't take an Einstein to work out that busty Brianna had joined her mother-in-law's 'I hate Amber' club.

She forced herself to smile when all she felt like

doing was screaming. 'Yes, that's right. We're very happy.' She almost cringed at her last comment, wondering why she felt compelled to validate her marriage to this bimbo.

The brunette wrinkled her pert little nose. 'Lucky you. I miss Steven.'

Amber gripped the counter before she did something stupid, such as tear the other woman's eyes out.

Thankfully, her mother-in-law stepped in. 'This place is so quaint.' However, her next words chilled Amber to the bone. 'It should keep you amused when Steven's attention wanders.' With that, she smiled a beatific smile at Brianna, leaving little to Amber's imagination. 'A pity you won't be joining us tonight, Amber. It promises to be a night to remember.'

Nodding at Brianna, Mrs. Rockwell opened the door and the women exited together, leaving Amber with a nauseous feeling in her gut that had nothing to do with morning sickness. The encounter with the poisonous old dragon and her sidekick had left her drained, and to make matters worse she had no idea what they were talking about.

Tonight? What was that about? Steve had begged off the celebratory dinner for her shop's opening citing business. She'd let him off the hook with the proviso that they held a private celebration in their bedroom when he returned home. Not just for the opening of *Harmony*, but also for the news she knew would thrill him.

And now she discovered that he'd lied to her. So much for honesty; Steve had given her hell after her meeting with that property developer, ranting and raving about trust in a marriage. Too bad her holier-than-thou husband didn't practise what he preached; tonight he was meeting up with an old girlfriend and his mother, who seemed hell-bent on destroying their marriage.

Great. Just great.

No amount of tending to her chakras would soothe her soul today. There was only one way to face trouble of this proportion and that was head-on.

Nothing like gate-crashing a party. And Amber had every intention of being the third woman to join her husband's little gathering tonight.

CHAPTER EIGHT

STEVE hated lying to Amber. He'd come so close to telling her about his promise to his grandmother, only to renege at the last minute. If he told her about his need for an heir to secure Ethel's fortune, and the reason why, his wife would divorce him quicker than the few days it had taken him to fall for her in the first place.

And he'd fallen hard, no doubt about that. Once he'd let go of his initial reservations she'd blossomed under his attentions, leaving him with a strange ache in the vicinity of his heart whenever she wasn't around. Not that he was stupid enough to confuse caring with love. The emotions she elicited in him were based on mutual respect, liking, and a rampaging lust that shook him in its intensity.

Now all they needed was a baby to seal their union and he would be the happiest man alive. The thought of a beautiful little girl who looked just like her mother clutched at his heart in a way he'd never thought possible. He would bestow all the love he could on his child, no doubt about it. No child of his would ever feel unwanted or unloved, as he had.

Besides, he needed an heir; there was no way his

mother would ever see a penny of his grandmother's fortune, not while he still lived and breathed.

He cringed at the thought of his mother. He'd lied to Amber about that too, saying he couldn't make it tonight due to business. In reality, he hadn't wanted to subject his wife to his mother's vitriol again, so he'd invented the excuse of a business dinner rather than ask Amber to accompany them to the fashion parade. He wanted to nurture Amber, not drive her away, and his mother had the power to do just that.

The intercom on his desk buzzed. 'Your mother on line two, Mr Rockwell.'

He sighed in resignation. He really shouldn't think of his mother. Whenever he did, she materialised. 'Put her through then call it a day, Chelsea.'

'Thanks, Mr Rockwell. See you in the morning.'

He steeled himself for the dulcet tones of his mother.

'Steven, what are you still doing at the office? Aren't you ready yet?'

He glanced at his watch, wondering if he had time to stop for a fortifying pint on the way to the Convention Centre.

As he heard the impatient clickety-clack of his mother's manicured nails, he knew it would take a keg or two to give him the forbearance to last an entire evening in her company. 'I said I'd be there at seven, Mother. What's your problem?'

'No problem, darling. I just have a surprise for you, that's all.'

He frowned and signed off on the last document on his desk. 'You know I hate surprises.'

Her laughter grated on his already stretched-to-breaking-point nerves. 'Trust me, Steven. You'll love this one.'

Trust his mother? He'd given up on that fairy tale a long time ago. 'See you at seven. And don't plan on a post-parade supper. I'm heading home to my wife afterwards.'

He didn't like her murmured, 'We'll see,' as he punched the disconnect button.

Amber lay back in the Jacuzzi and closed her eyes, savouring the water jets that pounded her weary flesh. It had been a long day, with inquisitive customers streaming into *Harmony* till closing time. She'd sold close to three thousand dollars' worth of stock, more than triple her expectations for the first week. Her dream had become a reality.

Well, at least one of them.

As for her happily-ever-after fantasy, that had taken a nosedive around the time the mother-in-law from hell and her offsider had entered her domain today. And had been firmly cemented in the delusional pile of discarded dreams just half an hour ago, when her lying husband had rung to confirm he'd be home late tonight. He'd even had the cheek to ask her to wait up for him!

She'd show him. Oh, yeah, she had it all planned out, starting with the daring designer dress she'd purchased on the way home and ending with a confrontation at the Convention Centre tonight.

It hadn't been too difficult discovering his plans. All she'd done was ring his helpful secretary and ask for the address of tonight's function, feigning a poor memory due to all the excitement of *Harmony's* opening and saying she wanted to surprise Steve, who had thought she wouldn't be able to make it. Chelsea had come through with flying colours, saying she would ring and leave Amber's name at the door, as the Magic Million's fashion parade was always a sell-out.

Now all she had to do was turn up and watch the fireworks unfold. If her husband had any thoughts of straying she'd give him a send-off he'd never forget.

Steve tugged at his bow-tie, wishing he could exchange the tux for one of the loose cotton shirts Amber had procured for him all the way from India. He wore suits every day, despite the cloying heat, and couldn't wait to get home and strip off. Which usually had more than one advantage…

'Darling, you made it. Right on time too.' His mother minced across the crowded foyer in three-inch heels, wearing a black sequinned sheath.

'I said I'd be here.' He couldn't help sounding petulant. She always brought out that trait in him, not to mention the overriding fact that he would

rather be home right now, cuddling up to his luscious wife and her welcoming curves.

'I'm so glad you are. Remember that surprise I
told you about?' His mother's eyes gleamed, their
cold, calculated sparkle almost but not quite rival-
ling the exquisite diamonds dangling from her ears
and encircling her throat.

'Cut to the chase, Mother. What's all this about?'

He fiddled with his wedding band, rolling it between his thumb and index finger. It was an action
he caught himself doing more and more these days,
and he found it strangely calming in his world of
never-ending problems.

'This is your surprise.' She waved a hand towards
the door. 'Enjoy, darling.'

Steve gaped as the woman he'd dubbed the Ice
Princess stalked across the foyer in a red dress that
left little to the imagination. Slashed to the waist in
front, it displayed her siliconed breasts to perfection.

'Hello, Steven. Long time no see.' She ran a
talon, painted the same red as her dress, down his
cheek.

'Well, well. So there's been a thaw.' He stepped
away from Brianna, wondering what he'd ever seen
in her.

She pouted, the glossy lipstick reminding him of
a blood slick. The description fitted well, as he knew
she could be a blood-sucking vampire, out for every
cent of his wealth she could lay her money-grubbing
hands on.

'Don't be like that, Steven. We had some good times together.' She leaned into him, doing her utmost to press her obvious enhancements against him.

'*Had* being the operative word, Brianna. In case you didn't know, I'm married now. Happily married.' He wished he hadn't added it as an afterthought.

'So?' The whispered word hung in the air between them, making him despise her all the more.

'Back off, Bree. I'm not interested.' He plucked her hand off his coat-sleeve and dropped it like a piece of unwanted rubbish.

Her mask peeled away before his eyes, leaving the chilly façade he'd grown accustomed to towards the end of their relationship. 'Your loss, yet again. You always were a poor judge of character, Steven. Looks like nothing's changed.'

He sensed some hidden meaning behind her frosty words. 'What are you talking about?'

Her upper lip curled in familiar derision. 'Your trashy wife.' She jabbed him with a long-nailed finger. 'You ditch me, the best thing that ever happened to you, for some carnival tramp? Poor you.'

Steve took a deep breath, willing his rage to subside. He'd never experienced such an all-consuming tidal wave of fury, and if he wasn't careful it would obliterate every ounce of decency he possessed. Rather than focusing it on the surly cow in front of him, he turned around and walked away, in search of the woman who had put him in this predicament in the first place.

Spotting his mother talking to one of the event organisers, he strode across the room. Grabbing her arm, he bent low and whispered in her ear. 'We need to talk. *Now.*'

She looked up at him with startled eyes.

Rage ran ice-cold in his veins. 'I mean it, Mother. Come with me or you'll regret it. I'll embarrass you right here and now, in front of all your phoney society parasites.'

His mother had class, he'd give her that much. Rather than coming apart at the seams, as most women would have done when faced with his fury, she lifted her head a fraction, nodded at her cronies and followed him.

'You're hurting me, Steven,' she said, as he half-pulled, half-dragged her across the foyer to a small room partitioned off by heavy drapes.

'And that's only the start, Mother.'

He dropped her arm and pulled the curtain across, cutting them off from prying eyes before turning to look at the woman who had spawned him and whom he despised. 'What the hell were you thinking, bringing Brianna here? And what did you tell her about Amber?'

His mother folded her arms and tried to stare him down. 'I'm trying to help you, Steven.'

'This kind of help I can do without.' His voice

had risen several octaves till he was almost shouting, and his mother's wince gave him a momentary satisfaction.

'Keep your voice down. Rockwells don't shout.'

'No, we don't.' He unclenched his fists before he punched a hole in the wall. 'We prefer to screw up our lives with silences, by holding back emotions, by locking our feelings away in the precious family vault. Much healthier.'

'Don't be ridiculous. Thanks to your upbringing, you've turned out just fine.' She paused, as if for effect. 'Apart from your judgement in women, that is.'

Something inside him snapped. 'That's it, Mother. It's over. I don't want to see you or hear from you ever again. You got that? As far as I'm concerned, I don't have a mother.'

Amber had entered the foyer of the Convention Centre in time to see that bimbo Brianna drape herself over Steve, only to be pushed away. She'd almost rushed up to him then, ready to forgive him on the spot, when she'd seen the angry altercation with his mother. Reluctant to eavesdrop, but keen to see her nemesis put in her place, she'd followed them to the far side of the room, where they now raged behind closed curtains.

She peeked through, and was delighting in her snobby mother-in-law getting her comeuppance, when the woman in question looked up and spotted her.

Rather than acknowledging her, Georgia Rockwell lifted her head and stared pointedly at her son. 'You can denounce me all you want, Steven, but it doesn't change the facts.'

Steve ran his hand through his hair and Amber yearned to rush in and smooth the ruffled spikes down. 'I've had enough of your interference to last me a lifetime. Get out. I'm not interested in anything else you have to say.'

'I know why you pulled that little tramp out of the gutter and married her.' Her mother-in-law stared straight at her, daring her to step forward.

A potent combination of shock and anger rooted Amber to the spot. Besides, she wanted to hear her husband send his mother packing once and for all.

'You know nothing. I said get the hell out of my life!' If the loud techno music for the parade hadn't started at that moment, every one of the patrons would have heard Steve's bellow.

Once again, Georgia Rockwell fixed Amber with a stare. 'Come, now, Steven. We both know the only reason you married that guttersnipe was to produce an heir for Ethel's fortune. And she was the only one stupid enough to fall for your routine. Or was your money an added incentive?'

Amber reeled from her mother-in-law's outlandish accusation. Steve didn't need an heir. Heck, at the start of their marriage he hadn't even mentioned children. She had been the one to stop taking the Pill once his attitude towards her changed.

Suddenly a nasty memory insinuated its way into her thoughts; Steve's quick negative shake of the head to his grandmother at the hope in her rheumy eyes that Amber could be pregnant. And, later, his strange eagerness when they had discussed children and his urging her to stop taking contraceptives.

Lord, no. It couldn't be true. Surely his attitude towards her had changed out of love, not some ploy to butter her up to produce an heir to the disgusting Rockwell wealth?

'How did you find out?'

And with those five little words uttered by the man she had grown to love more than life itself her world came crashing down.

Clutching her belly to protect her unborn child, she turned away from her mother-in-law's triumphant grin and stumbled towards the entrance. Once outside, she leaned against a wall and fought the rising sobs, taking in great gulps of air to quell the devastation. Her teeth started to chatter, despite the balmy evening, as shock set in.

Need to get home, she thought, hailing a passing taxi. Only problem was, home wasn't in Brisbane. She needed to escape the city and get back to her van, the only refuge in the world that had kept her safe from the overwhelming feelings of loss and grief that had plagued her eleven years ago when her mum died and had just returned in full force.

'You all right, lady?' The taxi driver peered at her through the rear-vision mirror.

She nodded, knowing that nothing would ever be all right again.

Steve unlocked the front door, operating on autopilot as a bone-deep weariness settled on his soul. He yearned for Amber's arms to wrap around him and soothe away all the nasty memories of the fight with his mother. Though he'd always despised her, he'd never known the depth of her evil till tonight. Somehow she'd guessed at his original motivation for marrying Amber, and he'd unwittingly confirmed it. However, he'd be damned if he let the old barracuda know how he felt about his wife now.

He answered to no one about his feelings, especially as he didn't know exactly what they were himself.

'Sweetheart, I'm home,' he called out, wondering why all the lights were out bar one. As he felt his way along the wall towards the switch, he stubbed his foot against a solid object that didn't belong there.

Muttering curses under his breath, he flicked the switch, flooding the room with light. He looked down at the offending object, surprised to see it was a suitcase—two of them, in fact.

'Amber? What's going on?' A sudden irrational panic lent urgency to his voice. Why had his wife packed her old decrepit cases?

'What does it look like?' Her voice came out of nowhere and he looked towards the stairs.

He struggled not to gape at the svelte vision in the black designer dress descending the staircase. She looked incredible, the dress showing her lush curves to perfection. She'd put on weight in the last few weeks and it gave her an added glow. Not that he'd told her he'd noticed her weight gain, he wasn't a complete moron.

'Wow. That's some dress. What's the occasion?'

She ignored him, sweeping into the lounge without looking at him. 'I'm leaving.'

'To become a model?' His attempt at humour fell flat as she picked up her handbag and rummaged through it. He wanted to reach out to her but her rigid posture screamed 'hands off'. He'd never seen her like this and it scared him. A lot.

'For good.' She finally turned to face him and he struggled to maintain composure. Her face looked blotchy, swollen, with her eyes red-rimmed. She hadn't just been crying, she'd been bawling.

'What's wrong, sweetheart?' He reached out to her, desperate to find out what had caused her pain and why she'd uttered those ridiculous words about leaving him.

'Don't touch me!' She backed away, holding her hands up. 'And I'm not your sweetheart.' She spat the words out, something akin to hate flashing in the depths of the eyes he'd grown to love.

Whack! It hit him like a subpoena out of the blue

and was just as unexpected. It wasn't only her eyes he loved. He loved all of her, every exquisite inch, from the top of her stubborn blonde head to the tip of that infernal toe-ring. And he realised it at a time like this, when his wife was on the verge of some kind of breakdown.

'I don't understand.' He opened his palms to her in supplication. He'd never begged for anything in his life, but now he was close. He needed her to open up to him, to tell him what was bothering her. For a man used to being in control, he didn't like feeling this helpless.

'That makes two of us.' The tears gleamed in her eyes, highlighting the golden flecks. 'I'll never forgive you for this. Ever.'

Her words pierced him as he struggled to grasp where they had come from. 'What have I done?'

As she shook her head from side to side tears trickled down her cheeks, making him feel like a bastard, though for the life of him he couldn't figure out why. 'Tell me!'

'Don't shout at me like I'm a child.' Her hands slid around her belly, and suddenly, he knew.

My God, she's pregnant.

He leaned against the wall for support, the realisation flooring him as a surge of paternal joy swept through him, swift and sharp. Was that what was behind her irrational behaviour? Fear of the unknown? Or, dared he say it, hormones?

'Amber, why didn't you tell me?'

She glared at him, clasping her arms firmer around her belly. 'Tell you what?'

'You're carrying my child.' He allowed his face to dissolve into a tentative smile, hoping it would reassure her of his feelings about the pregnancy. It didn't.

She tilted her head up in the familiar defiant gesture he'd grown to be wary of. 'You're wrong. This is *my* child, and you, your twisted mother and your sick grandmother aren't going to get your hands on him or her.'

Blood drained from his head and for a second he thought he would faint for the first time in his life. Dammit, she knew. His mother must have told Amber about her suspicions and his wife believed her.

Thankfully, his lightning-quick thinking processes asserted themselves; it wasn't as bad as he had first thought. All he had to do was deny his mother's accusations and profess his love for her. Who would she believe? His mother, whom she couldn't stand, or him?

'I don't know what Mother told you, but it's a pack of lies. I'm rapt that you're pregnant, and I can't wait to welcome our child into the world.' He paused, the growing look of horror on her face not inspiring him much. 'There's something else I need to tell you. I love you.'

To his amazement, she threw her head back and laughed, a haunting, hysterical sound that raised the hairs on the back of his neck, before she clapped. 'Great performance. Shame about the delivery.'

She walked towards him, tottering on high heels. 'Words are cheap, hotshot.' She punctuated each word with a jab at his chest. 'Love? You wouldn't know the meaning of the word, even if it came up and bit you on your filthy-rich butt! As for wanting this baby, I just bet you do. After all, what better way to add to your millions than by producing an heir to inherit Granny's fortune?'

He sank into the nearest chair, floundering for something, anything, to allay her fears. 'It's not what you think.'

'Don't lie to me!' she yelled, a bright crimson flushing her cheeks. 'I know! I heard you!'

Oh, God. She'd been at the Convention Centre; that was why she was dressed up. And she'd probably heard every damning word of his conversation with his mother.

'Don't do this, Amber. I can explain…' He trailed off at the revulsion in her face, a deep-seated fear clutching at his heart at the thought of losing the most important thing that had ever happened to him.

'Save it for someone who cares.'

She didn't look back as she picked up her battered cases, walked out through the door and slammed it behind her.

Steve dropped his head in his hands, wishing he could run after her. However, his wife was right; words were cheap. And, the way she must be feeling right now, nothing he could say would convince her of the truth.

The truth. Hell, he loved her, and the life-changing revelation had to hit him at a time like this.

He *had* to show her how much she meant to him, with actions rather than words. Starting tomorrow.

CHAPTER NINE

AMBER couldn't return to the carnival and the sanctity of her caravan, despite every self-preservation mechanism she possessed screaming for her to do just that. She had a business to run and there was no way she'd give her soon-to-be ex-husband any ammunition to use against her like saying she couldn't look after a newly opened shop so how could she care for a baby?

A baby. For the first time in two hours she smiled and hugged her stomach. It didn't matter that her life was crumbling around her ears, she still had the one thing that she'd always wanted and no one could take it away from her.

Suddenly a flicker of doubt flashed through her brain. The Rockwells were richer than rich, and Steve was a top-class lawyer. What if they tried to take this baby away from her by dragging her through the courts? They could afford a long and lengthy legal battle, she couldn't. They had the connections to make anything happen, she didn't. And what if Steve reneged on the financing for *Harmony*, depriving her of an income to support her child?

The questions she didn't want to acknowledge, let alone answer, whirled through her mind as she collapsed onto the hotel bed and closed her eyes, wishing she could shut out her husband's image.

He'd said he loved her. *Jerk!*

After months of waiting and hoping, he'd said the three little words she'd longed to hear yet it meant nothing. She knew he would have said anything to get his hands on their baby and his grandmother's fortune. What sort of a sicko was he anyway, to use another human being to further his own ends?

Trying to blot out the pain that threatened to shatter her heart into a million pieces, Amber turned onto her side, curled into a foetal position and cried herself to sleep.

Steve needed to talk to someone. Badly. And the only person he trusted in the world was his grandmother. He'd booked a flight to Melbourne as soon as Amber had left last night, needing to do something other than curse his own stupidity at letting the best thing that had ever happened to him slip right through his fumbling fingers.

As the two-hour flight from Brisbane to Melbourne drew to a close, he sat back in his business-class seat and pondered his dilemma. Technically, his grandmother wasn't the only person he'd grown to trust. Amber had insinuated her lively presence into his life and knocked down every one of his defences, bar one.

If only he'd recognised his feelings earlier he could have told her the truth behind his grandmother's fortune and why he had to have it. She would have understood; hell, she would probably have helped him do what he had to do. God, he'd been a fool. For someone with an outstanding IQ, he sure knew diddly-squat when it came to matters of the heart.

And he was through blaming his mother for the way he'd turned out; he controlled his own emotions now. So what if his mother had been a cold-hearted bitch and still was? He'd given up on her a long time ago. Amber was another matter entirely…

He remembered these thoughts as he knocked on the door to his grandmother's bedroom an hour later.

'Come in.'

Taking a deep breath, he opened the door, bracing himself for the worst. It had been several weeks since he'd seen his grandmother and she'd looked terrible the last time, the ravaging cancer leaving her pale and gaunt. 'Hi, Gran. It's me.'

Surprisingly, Ethel St John sat upright, propped by a mountain of pillows, her eagle stare as acute as ever. 'So, what have you done this time, my boy?'

He bent down and kissed her wrinkly cheek, marvelling at how well she looked. 'Why can't a man just pay a visit to his grandmother without having done something?'

She waggled a bony finger at him. 'I may be dying but I'm not senile. You've got that look, Steven. The one you always had when one of your infamous chemistry experiments blew up in your face. Now, sit and tell me all about it.'

He perched on the edge of her bed. 'I will, but first tell me how you're feeling. You're looking much better.'

In fact, her appearance had startled him. Her cheeks were more filled out than he'd seen in a long time, with a tinge of healthy colour.

She waved her hand in a dismissive gesture. 'Codswallop! Must be those health pills I'm taking. Can't cure me, but they'll make sure I look damn good in my casket. Now, tell me what's going on.'

Her attitude amazed him; she'd accepted death with the aplomb she'd shown her entire life. And, true to form, she was still as sharp as a packet full of razorblades.

'It's about Amber—'

'Is she pregnant?' Ethel interrupted, a shrewd gleam behind her cataracts.

He nodded, wondering how he could tell his grandmother that, though his wife carried his child, she probably wouldn't speak to him ever again.

'Well done, my boy. I knew you could do it. Now I can die happy.'

'Gran, there's more.'

She ignored his concerns. 'There always is with you Rockwells. Thank goodness your mother had the good sense to have you, otherwise what would have happened to the St John fortune? It's about the only thing she's done right in her miserable life. When's the baby due?'

'I'm not sure.'

'*What?* You don't know when your own child is to be born? What sort of a father are you?' Her look of incredulity shook him.

'Oh, about the same type of husband I am. Rotten.' He said it as a matter of fact, wishing it wasn't true. He'd never had a hankering to be married, but now that he'd had a taste of it he'd become addicted. And he had no intention of attending Divorcees Anonymous.

Her eyes narrowed, just as they had the time he'd put snails in her bed about twenty years ago. 'You've hurt that nice young woman, haven't you? And probably botched your marriage in the process.'

He had the grace to look sheepish. 'Something like that. I didn't tell her about the proviso in your will and she found out from Mother.'

His grandmother paled. 'Oh, no. How could you be so stupid?'

He'd backed himself into a corner and the only way to get out was to come clean. About all of it. 'I didn't love Amber at the start; that's why I didn't tell her.'

'But why did you marry her?' Confusion marred his grandmother's face and he wished he didn't have to put her through this.

He'd screwed up, big-time.

'Mother told me you didn't have long to live, so

I wanted to give you the one thing you wanted before you...' He couldn't bring himself to say the word 'died'. 'I liked Amber, she needed me as much as I needed her, so we married.'

'What do you mean, she needed you?' Typical Gran, she let nothing go through to the keeper.

He sighed, knowing she wouldn't like this part, not one little bit. 'Her father's business needed money to stay open, so I provided it. I knew she could have kids, so—'

'You *bought* her? Like some brood mare?' The disgust on her face made him want to hide out in the pool-house, as he'd used to do as a six-year-old after one of her tongue-lashings. 'What were you thinking?'

He shook his head, wishing he didn't have to have this conversation. 'I wasn't.'

'Is the money that important to you, Steven?'

'Hell, no!'

'Then why?' The pain he heard in his grandmother's voice tore him apart.

'I wanted to make you happy, to give you one tenth of the happiness you gave to me growing up. If you could've just seen your great-grandchild, surely it would've made everything easier?' He waved towards the stack of pill bottles, the commode, the oxygen tank standing like a lone soldier in the corner of the room.

She placed a hand over his, offering comfort as she always had. 'Darling, hearing your plans for my money made me happier than you could possibly imagine. I don't need to see my great-grandchild to know you'd do the right thing in setting up a trust fund and using my money to open up a cancer facility for kids. You've always made me proud of you, and I see no reason why that would change when I'm gone.'

He gripped his grandmother's hand, just as he had the first time she'd taken him to kindergarten. 'I've made a mess of things, haven't I?'

She squeezed his hand. 'Not with me. But I think there's a certain young lady who needs to hear all of this.'

'What if she won't listen?'

Hell, she'd laughed when he'd said he loved her. Why would she believe the rest of what he had to tell her?

'If she loves you, she'll listen. Besides, aren't you some hotshot lawyer? Use your negotiating skills.'

Ethel had been so proud of him the day he'd graduated; she'd never belittled his choice of career, or the fact he'd needed to establish his own wealth. Pity his mother couldn't be the same. Not that it mattered any more; once his mother discovered their plans for Ethel's money she'd disown him. Thank God.

'Amber calls me that.'

'What?'

'Hotshot.' He remembered the first time she'd

called him that, full of spunk and sass. God, how he loved her.

And what if his grandmother was right and his wife did love him? Though he couldn't be sure, he knew she shared his passion inside the bedroom, and seemed to genuinely like him outside of it, but did that equate to love? Even after he'd told her to keep the dreaded 'L' word out of their marriage?

His grandmother chuckled. 'I like the girl. Now, go get her.'

When it came to the indefatigable Ethel St John, he always did as he was told.

Amber locked the front door and pulled down the blinds. It had been a long day in the shop. Once again curious customers had filed in, checking out the merchandise and spending a small fortune. Even her dad had dropped by, saying he had business in town, but she knew better. He hated the fifty-minute drive from the Gold Coast to Brisbane and avoided it at all costs, conducting all his business via the phone or internet, so she'd known he'd come to check up on her.

Colin Lawrence looked like a new man, thanks to the Rockwell cash injection that had saved the carnival. Luckily, her dad had insisted on signing a proper contract for the finance; had he had some inkling that her marriage would end this way and didn't want to jeopardise his business? If so, he'd been smarter than she had, though she couldn't bring herself to tell him the truth just yet.

She'd put on a brave face, blaming her strained, tired look on *Harmony*'s opening, and thankfully he'd believed her. After wishing her well, and purchasing a small vial of lavender oil which he occasionally burned for relaxation after years of coaxing from her, he left the shop.

Her brave façade had slowly waned over the day, though she'd been thankful for the hectic pace that kept her mind from drifting to her predicament. She'd never wanted to be a single mother, yet here she was, about to become just that. As for divorce— that only happened to other people who didn't want to work at keeping their marriage alive, or so she had foolishly thought.

A single tear rolled down her cheek and she brushed it away angrily. She'd cried enough tears last night to fill the Pacific Ocean and had sworn that she wouldn't wallow in self-pity any more. She had a business to run, a baby to nurture and a future that could become anything she wanted to make it. Then why did she feel as if her chakras were way out of sync?

A loud banging on the front door interrupted her musings.

'We're closed,' she called out, but the noise continued.

'OK, OK, hold your horses.'

As she peeked through the blind she saw the last

man she expected or wanted to see. And, what was worse, her traitorous heart leapt at the sight of him, looking a million dollars in his trademark suit.

'Amber, we need to talk.' Typically, Steve made it sound like an order, not a request.

She dropped the blind and turned away from the door, leaning against it. 'Go away. I have nothing to say to you.'

'Well, I have plenty to say to you, so open this door. Now.'

She hated being controlled almost as much as she hated being lied to—two things her husband seemed to excel at. Folding her arms across her chest, she shouted, 'Make me.'

'Don't push me, Amber.' His voice had dropped low, dangerously so. Not that she cared. What could he do to her now? He'd already ripped her heart out.

'Why not? It's not like you care or anything.' Amber knew she sounded petulant; in fact, she sounded downright childish. She should be ranting and raving like a proper adult, not pouting like some jilted teenager.

However, that one glimpse of Steve through the blinds had undermined all her intentions to push him away. He looked haggard, his steel-grey eyes ringed by dark circles, day-old stubble covering his jaw and his tie askew, with the top button of his shirt undone. She always knew he was rattled when he undid his top button, for her suave husband, the consummate

professional, wouldn't be caught dead looking anything less than immaculate.

He rattled the doorknob. 'Amber, let me in. We
can't have this conversation through a door.' Almost
as an afterthought, he added, 'Please?'

His uncertainty tugged at her heartstrings. He
must *really* be feeling vulnerable to say the magical
'P' word.

Against her better judgement, she unlocked the
door, stuck her head out and tried to ignore the
funny stabbing sensation in her heart. 'This is a
waste of time.'

He ran a hand through his hair and she resisted
the urge to smooth it down. 'I don't think so.'

Amber tried to hide her surprise; not only was his
top button undone but he'd also forgotten his tie-
pin, and his favourite pen had leaked in the top
pocket. Dire straits for her perfectionist husband. His
ragged appearance sent a flare of hope piercing
through her. Maybe she meant more to him than a
means to an end?

As he reached for her, she held up a hand. 'Before
you set foot in here, let's establish ground rules.
Number one, you will not order me around. Number
two, you will not try to control my life. And, most
importantly, number three, you will walk out of this
shop at the end and respect my decision. Is that understood?'

His eyes darkened and his lips compressed into a

thin line, but he didn't protest. 'Your call. Can I come in now?'

Another surprise—he didn't argue and he'd agreed to all her terms. He must be feeling a heck of a lot worse than she'd first thought. Good. Why should she be the only one to suffer?

She walked behind the counter and sat on a stool, feeling somewhat safer with the wide glass-topped bench between them. Though her head followed logic, her body had always been lousy at keeping up when it came to this man, and she didn't need him undermining her defences right now with a simple touch. For that was all it would probably take for her to tumble into his arms like some pathetic loser.

She sat on her hands to stop them fidgeting; he didn't need to know how nervous she felt. 'Well? What's so profound that you have to come inside to say it?'

Confusion marred his powerful features as he stared at the shelf behind her. 'Where are all the cushions?'

Oh, no. If he couldn't undermine her with his touch, he would do it with words. By referring to the multicoloured cushions they had made love on he resurrected a host of scorching memories, starting with the way he'd stripped her, kissed and licked his way down her body, before making her world explode—twice.

Blinking rapidly to erase the vivid images that

had flickered across her mind like a rerun of a classic movie, she glared at him. 'We don't stock *used* merchandise in this store. Which is funny, considering *I* still work here.'

His jaw clenched. 'I didn't use you, Amber.'

'Really? Then what would you call it?' She tapped a finger against her temple, as if pondering the answer. 'Oh yeah, that's right. You married me for *love*.'

'Things change. People change. I…'

'Give me a break! The great Steve Rockwell, change? Not likely. You use people all the time, whether it be for business or pleasure.' She slid off the stool and planted both hands on the counter in front of her. 'So which one was I, hotshot?'

He strode across the shop, seemingly intent on grabbing her. She yelped and sidled farther behind the counter, thankful for its width.

He leaned forward but couldn't reach her. 'Stop it! We need to sort this out.'

'Correction. You need to talk, expecting me to listen. Well, too bad. We don't always get what we want.' She thrust her head up and blinked back tears, wishing she could have it all and knowing it would never happen.

'Amber, I'm warning you…'

She'd never seen him like this; he should have been madder than a prosecutor at a mistrial, yet he wasn't. In fact, by the gleam in his eye, she could have sworn he was enjoying himself.

'Ooh, poor little Stevie. What are you going to do? Spank me?'

'That does it!'

Before she could react, he'd vaulted the counter and had her pinned against the wall, all the breath knocked out of her.

'Let me go,' she gasped, wriggling like a hooked fish to escape his vice-like grip.

'Don't you ever quit fighting, woman?' He stepped into her, thrusting his lean, hard body against her and effectively stilling her writhing.

She should have shoved him away. She should have screamed and kicked and bitten her way out of his grasp. She should have told him his fortune, just as she'd promised the first time she'd laid eyes on him. But she didn't. Instead, she stopped fighting as a torrid wave of desire sizzled through her body, burning the last of her resistance and igniting a familiar fuse.

'Amber, look at me.'

Ignoring his command, and the palpitations of her heart, she shook her head from side to side, wishing she'd maintained her distance. Apart from the prickling contact of his hands against her bare skin, his signature aftershave enveloped her in a tantalising cloud, drowning out the potent combination of essential oils she'd been burning earlier.

'This won't solve anything,' she murmured, wishing her erratic pulse would calm down so she could hear herself think.

He tipped her chin up, forcing her to meet his gaze. 'Are you sure about that?'

He didn't give her a chance to answer before his lips covered hers in a blistering kiss.

She'd expected gentle coaxing, skilful cajoling; instead, she got a blazing mixture of lips and tongue, demanding compliance. Any thought of resistance fled as his kiss rendered her senseless, her wayward hormones enticing her to do all sorts of crazy things, like grab the front of his shirt, fumble with his buttons and shove the material aside till her palms lay flat against the hot, taut skin.

He broke the kiss for a second, to comb his fingers through her hair and stare deeply into her eyes. 'You know how I feel about you, and I want this baby more than anything. Can we start over?'

Fear lanced through her as he placed a hand on her belly. Lord, what had she been thinking? This had to be some kind of act; he'd come in here thinking he could blind her with sex and a few well-chosen words and she would fall back into his arms. No way.

She pushed against his chest, hard, and he staggered back, a ridiculous look of surprise on his face. 'It's finished, Steve. Now, get the hell out of my life.'

He looked dazed, staring at her as if she'd gone mad. 'But what about the baby?'

She should have known. That was all he cared about—producing an heir to inherit Granny's fortune. If he'd plied her with apologies, with whispered words of reassurance or professed his undying love, she might have wavered.

However, her calculating husband had just sealed his fate, his words reinforcing the fact that he saw her as an incubator and nothing else. Her head spun as a wave of unbearable pain washed over her. She needed to escape—now.

Suddenly she knew how to get rid of the man who stood in front of her, breaking her heart and shattering her dreams all over again.

'There is no baby.' Though she wasn't religious, she said a silent prayer, wishing she wouldn't go to hell for telling such a monstrous lie.

His thunderous look had her gripping the shelf behind her for support and wishing that a gigantic hole would open up in the ground beneath her. *'What?'*

She turned away in the pretence of finding a tissue, unable to meet his stare. 'I made a mistake. Turned out that the stress of opening this place made me skip a period. No big deal.'

He made a strange, strangled sound and she looked around, shocked at the bleakness spreading across his face. 'You're wrong.'

'About what?' Tears welled as he continued to stare at her, his devastation more than she could handle right now.

'Everything.' His mouth was screwed in a disapproving line, his voice hoarse and strained. 'About it not being a big deal that there's no baby, about how I feel about you, about our marriage. You're wrong about it all.'

She took a steadying breath, needing to drive him away once and for all, before she broke down completely. She tilted her chin up and forced herself to look him directly in the eye.

'I'm sorry to disappoint you, Steve, but this baby-making factory has just closed down as far as you're concerned. Better luck next time. As for our marriage, you know I only married you for the money. Anything else you interpreted was pure fantasy. No hard feelings, huh?'

And just like that the man of her dreams cast a final stricken look in her direction and walked out of her life.

CHAPTER TEN

STEVE signed the final document, handing over full
control to Amber for the shop, and popped it into
an Express postbag. He didn't want any links to the
woman who had breezed into his life like a cyclone
and left behind a similar path of destruction.
Besides, the shop had been her baby from the start.

Baby.

He hadn't thought it could still hurt this much
after three months, yet the mere thought of the word
made his palms sweat. He'd pinned his hopes of
saving their marriage on their unborn child, though
Amber had had other ideas. The minute she'd told
him there was no baby he'd known his chances of
convincing her that he loved her were non-existent.
His one tenuous link to bind him to her had dis-
solved with her bombshell, along with his hopes to
present his grandmother with a great-grandchild before she died.

And then she'd sealed his fate with her comment
about marrying him for money. God, that had hurt.

He'd deluded himself, believing she felt a spark,
as he had at the beginning, when it had been his
wealth that had attracted her all along. She was just
like his mother, out for everything she could get.

163

And he despised her for it. Hell would freeze over before he loved a woman like that.

So he'd done the only thing possible and thrown himself headlong into his business, working maniacal hours and avoiding contact with everybody other than colleagues. He rang his grandmother weekly, though he hadn't plucked up the courage to tell her the truth yet. It would devastate her, and she had enough to cope with at the moment.

As for his mother, she hadn't spoken to him since their confrontation at the Convention Centre. Why would she, when he'd dashed her dreams of inheriting and subsequently squandering Ethel's millions?

He sealed the postbag, handling it like a bomb about to detonate. This was it. No more contact with Amber till he served her with divorce papers in nine months' time—a year to the day since their separation. He'd circled the date in red on his calendar, just in case he forgot.

Fat chance. There wasn't a day that went by that he didn't think about her, wondering what she was wearing, who she was seeing, and driving himself crazy in the process.

A knock on the door brought his attention back to the present. 'Come in.'

Luke Saunders, one of the criminal lawyers from the Sydney branch of Byrne and Associates, stuck his head around the door. 'Got a minute for an old mate?'

Steve waved him in. 'Hey, Saunders. What are you doing here?'

'I was in the area. Thought I'd drop in and see what you've done up here.' They shook hands and Luke surveyed the office. 'Not bad, Rockwell. Not bad at all. So, how's business?'

Steve indicated that Luke take a seat. 'Can't complain.'

'I hear you've been inundated. Burning the midnight oil, huh?'

'Byrne been opening his big trap again?'

Luke nodded. 'He did mention something about it. Thought it was unusual for a newly-wed to spend so much time at the office. You know how he was after he married Kara. Couldn't get out the door quick enough at the end of the day.'

Steve took a deep breath and unclenched his fists under the desk. Matt and Luke were the closest he had to friends, yet could he really divulge the truth to them?

Luke continued. 'Go on, spill your guts, Rockwell. I know something's bothering you.'

Making a split-second decision, Steve leaned back and clasped his hands behind his head. 'Amber and I are separated.'

He hated seeing the pity in Luke's eyes. 'That's too bad. Want to go out and get plastered?'

Steve shook his head, amazed that he felt like laughing; he hadn't done that in months. 'Wish it was that simple.'

'What happened?'

'I blew it. Big-time. We got married for all the wrong reasons, and by the time I'd worked it out it was too late.'

He paused, wondering why he couldn't have laid it all on the line like this for Amber, rather than skirting around the main issue—the fact that he loved her. The baby had been fantastic news, but it didn't matter if he didn't have her love.

'Now she doesn't want a bar of me and, thanks to a few choice words on her behalf, the feeling's entirely mutual.'

Luke shook his head. 'I know you, Rockwell. You can be pretty bloody stubborn. Not to mention demanding, controlling and an all-round pain in the ass. Are you sure there's nothing you can do?'

'Thanks for the character reference. Nice to know who your friends are at a time like this.'

Luke chuckled. 'Hey, I'm not the one buried in here, trying to score points with the boss.'

'I *am* the boss, in case you've forgotten.' Steve remembered how Luke had welcomed him into the firm after Jeff Byrne had appointed him as a partner, and had smoothed the way with Matt, who had coveted the position. They had been firm friends since, not that they saw much of each other these days.

'Anyway, enough about me. What are you doing in Brisbane? Anything to do with a woman?'

Steve had seen Luke in action with the opposite sex; women flocked to his friend, equating his blond, boyish looks with an easy-going, fun-loving guy who would stick around. They were right, to a point; Luke loved having fun, though with myriad beauties. He wasn't a stayer, a fact which most women didn't like a hell of a lot.

'Women!' Luke rolled his eyes. 'Give me a break. I'm up here to escape them, though I am staying with one at the moment.'

'This sounds interesting.' Steve wanted to hear Luke's story—anything to divert his mind away from his own dreary problems. 'What gives?'

'Don't get too excited. I'm staying with my younger sister and she's driving me mad, dragging me from one theme park to the next, then browsing through every shop between here and the Gold Coast. She's nuts! She even took me to some way-out hippy joint the other day and tried to drape me in crystals, saying I had a bad aura or some such crap. If it hadn't been for the babe behind the counter I'd've been out of there in a flash.'

A strange prickling awareness raised the hairs on Steve's neck. Needing not to appear too eager, he tried to pry more information out of his friend. 'You see babes everywhere you go. What was so special about this one?'

Luke's eyes lit up whenever he discussed women. 'Man, she was a stunner. Long blonde hair, loads of it that hung down her back, hazel eyes, and a bod that just wouldn't quit. Phew, the curves! And talk about big…' Luke used both hands to indicate breasts of Pamela Anderson proportion.

Steve quelled the urge to beat his friend into a pulp. Surely the woman he'd just described couldn't be Amber? Luke could have just outlined any number of women who lived up here; Queensland was brimming with well-stacked blondes with killer bodies.

Luke continued, oblivious to his thoughts. 'Pity she had a bun in the oven. I could've really gone for a looker like that.'

Luke's grin faded as Steve jumped to his feet.

'What was the name of the shop?' Steve strode around the desk and just stopped short of hauling Luke from the chair and shaking the answer out of him.

'Whoa! Calm down, big fella.' Luke paused, driving Steve's already skyrocketing blood pressure up another notch. 'Let me think…something to do with inner peace…uh…'

'Was it *Harmony*?' Steve held his breath, trying to maintain his cool. He'd never wanted to hear an affirmative answer so much in all his life, but if it was, what the hell was he going to do about it?

Luke snapped his fingers. 'Yeah, that's the one. Have you been there? What did you think of the babe?'

Steve didn't trust himself to hang around; he valued Luke's friendship too much for it to end in fisticuffs. Picking up his suit jacket from the back of his chair, he flung open the door. 'That *babe* happens to be my wife. And she has a lot of explaining to do.'

Steve slammed the door on his friend's gaping mouth.

Amber winced and rubbed her back. Standing on her feet all day wasn't conducive to carrying around an extra few kilos, precious as the cargo was. She had a feeling that sleeping on the cramped, saggy bed in her old caravan each night didn't help either. Oh, well, beggars couldn't be choosers. At least she had a place to sleep at night, which was more than could be said for a lot of single mothers these days.

'Knock, knock. Are you in, love?' Her dad opened the rusty aluminium door and let himself in.

'Hi, Dad.' She stood on tiptoe to kiss him on the cheek, just as she had as a little girl. She felt as if she regressed more and more into her childhood with every passing day; living in the van again, having her dad check up on her daily and her huge extended carnival family smothering her with concern.

'So, how are you feeling?'

Yeah, nothing had changed. And it was driving her round the twist.

'I'm fine, Dad. Stop fussing. Don't you have a business to run or something?' She filled the kettle, craving a cup of chamomile tea to soothe her frazzled nerves.

He sat down at the cramped table and she heaped coffee and three sugars into another cup, just the way he liked it. 'I wouldn't have a business if you hadn't gone off and wrecked your life because of me.'

Amber sighed and poured the boiling water, glad for something to do with her hands; it prevented them from wrapping around her father's neck and squeezing hard. 'We've had this conversation a thousand times before, Dad. I married Steve because I wanted to, not for the money. And this baby isn't a disaster, it's a godsend.'

Colin Lawrence didn't look convinced. 'Then why hasn't this child got two parents instead of an overworked, half-starved one?'

She handed him the coffee and sat opposite him. 'Half-starved? I'm as big as the side of a house! I've even had to take my belly-button ring out.'

Her dad rolled his eyes. 'Thank goodness for small mercies. You could take that poor child's eye out with that horrid thing.'

'Get with it, Dad.' She managed a weak smile to show him that she cared despite his paternal nagging.

He sipped his coffee and gave a satisfied sigh. 'Hey, how much more "with it" can I get? I've just been reading up on which star sign my grandchild's going to be born under. You know, all those rising moons and cusps and things?'

'Really?' She couldn't believe her ears.

Her dad grinned, the laughter-lines around his eyes crinkling into their familiar pattern. 'Nah, just kidding, love.'

She joined in his laughter. 'Thanks, Dad. For everything.'

And she meant it; her father had opened his welcoming arms the night she'd knocked on his door and told him the whole sorry tale about her split with Steve.

Not that she'd told him everything—just enough to reassure him that she would be fine and that he was not to contact her husband under any circumstances. She'd made him promise and, true to his word, he'd left the 'scumbag, good-for-nothing lawyer' alone, as he'd labelled her ex.

Colin drained the rest of his coffee in a few gulps and stood up, appearing uncomfortable with her gratitude. 'Thanks for the cuppa, love. Get some rest and I'll see you tomorrow.'

'OK. Bye.' She waved at her dad and sipped her tea, wondering when the papers for the shop would arrive.

Steve had corresponded with her via several documents that had scared her witless at the start, till she'd realised that he wasn't trying to frighten her with legalities but was actually attempting to finalise her ownership of *Harmony*. She expected the final contract any day now and couldn't wait; the shop would be her son or daughter's trust fund one day, and she had to make it legally hers to ensure her child had a secure future.

Unlike hers. These days she drifted from one day to the next, not sure what the future held and not particularly caring. Her pain at losing Steve was still too acute, too raw, and she had a hard enough time faking smiles for her customers and allaying her father's fears to even think about what the next day might bring.

She barely registered the door to the van opening as she quashed the rising tide of panic that threatened to swamp her whenever she thought about a future without the one man who had rocked her world.

'Did you forget something, Dad?' She looked up and almost upended her cup as Steve's broad-shouldered silhouette blocked out the setting sun.

Her first impulse, to fling herself headlong into his arms, took her by surprise. She should be running ten miles in the opposite direction, not wanting to snuggle into his arms and beg him to chase away all her doubts.

'What are you doing here?' she managed to say, while slinking down in the chair to hide her swollen belly behind the tablecloth, wishing her erratic heartbeat would calm down. How could he still affect her after all this time?

'Hello, Amber. I hear you've got some news for me.' He didn't wait to be invited into the van. Instead, he stooped his large frame and entered, slamming the door behind him so hard that the hinges rattled.

She'd envisaged this scene several times in her dreams, a happy reunion where Steve would sweep her into his arms, caress her belly and swear his undying and eternal love. Then, like now, she'd woken up. And the reality hurt more than she could possibly bear.

She lashed out, all the months of pent-up pain spilling over. Patting her large stomach, she looked him straight in the eye. 'What makes you think it's yours?'

He covered the space between them in two strides and grabbed hold of her arm, almost dragging her to her feet.

'Quit lying to me. I want the truth and I want it now, damn you.'

Every tense line of his body radiated anger. She'd never seen him this mad and it scared her. Her lies had fuelled his fury; would he seek vengeance by taking away the one thing that mattered? Her teeth gnawed at her bottom lip; she wanted to fall into his arms, to tell him the truth, to let him soothe her pain. But there was too much at stake, and even the welcome contact of his grip and the familiarity of his steely gaze couldn't shake her conviction.

'You're hurting me. Let go,' she said, mustering every ounce of courage she possessed.

He dropped his hand and, stupidly, she missed his brief touch. 'Please, Amber.' His low words sounded like a plea. 'I need to know. I'm going insane here.' He thrust his hands in his pockets, drawing her attention to areas of his body she would rather have forgotten.

He looked irresistible, prime candidate for heart-throb of the year. And if the way her body was re-acting was any indication he wouldn't just win first prize, he would scoop the pool. Jacketless, the white business shirt moulded his chest as if it had been poured on, and she knew the multitude of sins it hid beneath: hard, rippling pecs and firm abs, good enough to eat. She salivated at the thought, won-dering how she could think of sex at a time like this. This man had the power to rip her world apart, to snatch the one thing that had become her reason for living—her precious baby.

'Remember that night at the shop, when I laid down the ground rules?' She had to ask him, though the last thing she wanted to do was recall that awful night, the night she'd lied to him and effectively ended any chance of happiness they possibly had.

He nodded, a wary look settling across his hand-some features.

She continued before she lost her nerve. 'You agreed to abide by my rules. Well, you said you would respect my decision and walk away at the end. So what are you doing here now?'

'I don't think rules count when lies are told. Especially not huge whoppers which damage peo-ple's lives.' He sank into the nearest chair and dropped his head in his hands. 'My God, Amber, what were you thinking?' He pressed his fingers against his eyes, not looking up at her, and for one horrifying moment she thought he was crying.

Something inside her snapped at that moment, her fragile defensive walls crashing down under the burden of the pain she'd caused, not just to herself but also to this man who had saved her father's business and, in doing so, alleviated her own guilt.

OK, so maybe he'd had some warped idea to use their child to inherit money? Was that so bad, considering she'd lied to him about their baby? And, worse, said she'd married him for his money?

As if in slow motion, she reached out and laid a tentative hand on his shoulder, wishing she could comfort him. And wishing she could take back every cruel word she'd ever spoken. 'Steve?'

He looked up, the desolate pain in his eyes cutting her more than anything he could say. 'I don't care that you don't love me. I don't care about the money. All I care about is raising my child, with all the love and guidance that I didn't have.'

She opened her mouth to correct him, to finally tell him the truth, that she loved him, but he cut in.

'Don't you get it? It was never about the money. Gran's will stipulated my child had to inherit her fortune to stop my mother from getting her greedy paws on it. Gran wouldn't leave it to me because she didn't think I'd be strong enough to hold out against my own mother, and she's probably right.

I've wanted Mother's approval my entire life, and if giving her more money meant obtaining it, who knows what I might have done? To make matters easier, Gran and I arranged that a trust fund would be set up, with most of the money to be used for a facility for kids with cancer.' He hadn't shrugged her hand off, and she could feel the tension in his shoulders. She gave him a reassuring squeeze though he didn't seem to notice.

'Maybe my motivation for having a child was mixed up at the start, but things changed. *You* changed everything, Amber. I knew you didn't love me, but I hoped that a child might bind you to me. You know, give you time to get to know me better and fall in love.' He shook his head from side to side. 'Guess I screwed up, huh?'

Her heart clutched with hope in the wake of his revelations. She'd misjudged her husband and it was time to make amends. She sat next to him and grabbed his hand, interlacing her fingers with his. 'I'm the screw-up here, not you.'

He looked a little uneasy, casting a doubtful glance in her direction. 'So the kid's mine?'

She nodded, wishing he would pull her into the curve of his arm and kiss her. She couldn't concentrate on what she had to say. The warmth of his hand was reviving cherished memories of how it had used to roam her body and set her alight.

Taking a steadying breath, she gripped his hand tighter. 'I lied to you. When I overheard your mother's accusations that night, and you confirmed them by asking how she'd found out, I couldn't think straight. I'd fallen in love with you and I'd thought you might reciprocate my feelings and that was why you were so keen to have a baby. When I found out the real reason, or so I thought, my mind shut down. I wanted to hurt you as much as you'd hurt me, that's why I told you there was no baby.'

He finally looked up, his wide-eyed expression of wonder giving her some hope. 'Back up a second. Did you just say you'd fallen in love with me?'

'Yeah. No accounting for taste, is there?' She gave him a watery smile, wiping away the tears with the back of her hand. 'I love you, you big, arrogant jerk!'

He pulled her towards him and smothered her in a bear hug that lasted an eternity. She snuggled into him, inhaling the familiar masculine scent that was pure Steve and wondering how she could have lived this long without him.

Just when she thought she couldn't breathe any more, he released his vice-like grip and peered into her face. 'Say it again.'

She stifled a grin. 'No. You'll get a big head. An even bigger one, that is.'

'God, how could we have been so stupid?'

He didn't give her a chance to answer, kissing her with an intensity that took her breath away. She responded with all the love her heart and soul possessed.

'Mmm, I've missed you,' Steve murmured, and as he drew Amber onto his lap and folded his arms around her, vowing that he would never let her go. He'd never known love could feel this good.

She wriggled against him and giggled. 'I can see that.'

'Hey! Haven't you done enough damage for one day? You're no lightweight.'

She hit him in the chest, a cheeky grin spreading over her face. In response, he captured her hand and placed it over his heart.

'See? The damage you've done here is irreparable. It'll never be the same again.' He leaned forward and rained gentle kisses on her nose, cheeks and mouth, saving the best for last as he nibbled on her delicious lips that had driven him crazy since the first time he saw her.

Tears misted her eyes as she drew his hand towards her protruding belly. 'Same here, hotshot.'

At that moment he felt a strange squirming beneath his hand and Amber gasped. 'Oh, my God. Did you feel that?'

He nodded, the wonder of the moment leaving him speechless.

'The baby kicked! Isn't that incredible?' Her eyes shone as her gaze flicked from his face to her belly and back again.

'Sure is, sweetheart. And so are you.' He kissed her again, wondering what their child would look like and hoping for a girl the spitting image of her mother.

A lone tear trickled down Amber's cheek and plopped onto his hand as she leaned forward and rubbed noses with him, Eskimo-style. 'So I guess this means you're ready to be a daddy?'

'What do you think?'

She cupped his cheek with her hand and gazed into his eyes. 'I think you're the greatest and I love you. Oh, and by the way, the tarot cards were right.'

He rolled his eyes. 'I thought you burned them after we married. After all, didn't they predict a tall, handsome stranger would walk into your life and sweep you off your feet? Surely once I appeared you didn't need them any more?'

She shook her head, the fresh floral fragrance of her hair wrapping him in a sensual cocoon. 'Why would I get rid of a foolproof method of predicting the future?'

He cuddled her closer, loving every inch of her, quirky nature and all. 'Well, as it happens, you have me for that now.' Turning her hand over, he peered into her palm. 'I see three kids…'

'Only three?'

He held up his other hand. 'Quiet! Don't disturb the master. I also see a man, an amazing man, with great looks and a body to die for—'

'Puh-lease!'

'—who will provide you with a lifetime of happiness and love. There. Think I'm any good?'

She smiled, brushed a kiss over his lips and whispered against the corner of his mouth, 'You're the best.'

EPILOGUE

STEVE and Amber barely made it, slipping into the back of the church just in time to witness the christening of Jessica Kate Byrne.

Their flight from Melbourne, where they'd been visiting his grandmother who was determinedly hanging on to life in order to see her first great-grandchild born, to Sydney hadn't been the problem. Steve marvelled at his wife's hormones, which hadn't abated as she entered her eighth month of pregnancy. Her enthusiasm in the bedroom, or the kitchen, or the lounge, had almost resulted in them missing the plane. Not that he was complaining.

As the guests mingled in the gardens following the service, Steve approached Luke and tapped him on the shoulder. 'Hey, Saunders. I think there's someone you might like to meet.'

His friend, trying to chat up a stunning brunette, turned around. 'Look, just because you're drowning in marital bliss, stop trying to set me up with…'

'Luke Saunders, meet Amber.' Steve paused for effect, enjoying the stunned expression on Luke's face. 'My wife.'

In a first, his friend seemed at a loss for words

181

before affecting the biggest, smoothest recovery of all time.

'Pleased to meet you, Amber. Steve's told me a lot about you.' He flashed her a killer smile, the same one Steve had seen him use on hundreds of gullible females before.

Amber had a slightly puzzled look on her face. 'Have we met before?'

Steve almost choked at the priceless expression on Luke's face, enjoying the rare spectacle of seeing the guy rattled.

Go ahead, Cool Hand Luke. Get yourself out of this one.

Before his friend could respond, Matt and Kara Byrne approached.

Matt slapped him on the back. 'Great to see you here, Rockwell. It's about time. A shame you've been hiding your lovely wife from us.' He turned to wink at Amber. 'I'm Matt and this gorgeous creature is my wife, Kara.'

Amber smiled. 'I've heard a lot about you. And congratulations. Jessica is beautiful.'

Matt stuck out his chest. 'Yes, she is. Takes after her mother, thank God.'

Kara rolled her eyes and linked arms with Amber. 'Come and help me with the drinks, Amber. There's too much testosterone around here.'

The women drifted off, leaving the three top lawyers at Byrne and Associates alone.

Matt thumped Steve on the arm. 'You sly old dog. You didn't tell me she was *that* stunning.'

'Oh? I'm surprised Saunders didn't fill you in.'

Steve glared meaningfully at Luke, enjoying his friend's discomfort. Though he'd forgiven him for the remarks he'd made about Amber, Steve wouldn't let him forget.

'Huh? What did I miss?' Matt's head swivelled between them. 'Come on, fellas, don't hold out on me.'

Luke shuffled his feet and looked down at the ground, appearing fascinated by two ants racing each other on a blade of grass. 'You're a jerk, Rockwell.'

Steve grinned. 'Go on, Saunders. Why don't you tell Byrne how you thought my wife was a hottie, especially her giant—'

'Enough!' Luke covered his ears with his hands. 'I've already apologised. Just leave it alone, will you?'

Matt chuckled. 'Sounds like we need to find you a woman, Saunders. The sooner the better, before you start cracking on to my wife too.'

'Ha, ha. You two are a real riot. Why don't you go off and play happy families and leave me the hell alone?'

Luke tried to look fierce for a moment, but ended up joining in the laughter. 'Besides, you're cramping my style. I didn't know Kara had so many cute friends.'

Steve glanced around at the crowd, noticing quite a few attractive women. Funnily enough, none of them captured his attention like his wife, who looked resplendent in matching maternity trousers and top, both made from a slinky black material that clung to her lush curves and outlined the swell of his child nestled deep in her belly. She looked up at that moment, as if sensing his gaze, and smiled at him across the lawn.

A strange tremor shot through him. His reaction to her beauty was almost visceral at times. God, he loved her, with every fibre of his being.

Matt nudged Luke. 'Don't look now, but Rockwell's making eyes at his wife. Doesn't it make you sick?'

Luke nodded. 'You both do. Later.' He strolled away, making a beeline for a group of rake-thin women in designer dresses.

Matt jerked his head towards the bevy of beauties. 'Do you miss it, Rockwell? The thrill of the chase?'

'Hell, no!'

Matt laughed and glanced over at Kara. 'Me either. Give me good old-fashioned lovin' any day.'

'Amen to that.' Steve's gaze drifted back to Amber, who beckoned him over. 'Duty calls, Byrne. Catch you later.'

Amber met him halfway across the lawn. 'My ears were burning. Singing my praises again?'

He chuckled. 'Loud and clear, sweetheart. What did you want?'

She stood on tiptoe and tried to press against him, no mean feat considering her girth.

'To tell you this.' She cupped a hand to his ear and whispered, 'I love you, hotshot.'

Reaching for her, he pulled her rounded body into his arms, eternally grateful for the joy she'd brought into his life.

Burying his face in the soft, fragrant skin between her neck and shoulder, he whispered, 'Mrs Rockwell, the feeling is entirely mutual.'

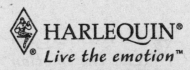

The world's bestselling romance series.

HARLEQUIN®
Presents

Seduction and Passion Guaranteed!

THE PRINCESS BRIDES

For duty, for money…for passion!

Discover a thrilling new trilogy from a rising star of Harlequin Presents®, Jane Porter!

Meet the Royals…

Chantal, Nicolette and Joelle are members of the blue-blooded Ducasse family. Step inside their sophisticated and glamorous world and watch as these beautiful princesses find they have to marry three international playboys—for duty, for money… and definitely for passion!

Don't miss

THE SULTAN'S BOUGHT BRIDE (#2418)
September 2004

THE GREEK'S ROYAL MISTRESS (#2424)
October 2004

THE ITALIAN'S VIRGIN PRINCESS (#2430)
November 2004

Pick up a Harlequin Presents® novel and you will enter a world of spine-tingling passion and provocative, tantalizing romance!

Available wherever Harlequin books are sold.

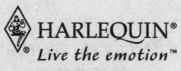

HARLEQUIN®
Live the emotion™

www.eHarlequin.com

HPPBJPOR

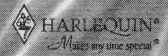

If you enjoyed what you just read,
then we've got an offer you can't resist!

Take 2 bestselling
love stories FREE!
Plus get a FREE surprise gift!

Clip this page and mail it to Harlequin Reader Service®

IN U.S.A.
3010 Walden Ave.
P.O. Box 1867
Buffalo, N.Y. 14240-1867

IN CANADA
P.O. Box 609
Fort Erie, Ontario
L2A 5X3

YES! Please send me 2 free Harlequin Romance® novels and my free surprise gift. After receiving them, if I don't wish to receive anymore, I can return the shipping statement marked cancel. If I don't cancel, I will receive 6 brand-new novels every month, before they're available in stores! In the U.S.A., bill me at the bargain price of $3.57 plus 25¢ shipping & handling per book and applicable sales tax, if any*. In Canada, bill me at the bargain price of $4.05 plus 25¢ shipping & handling per book and applicable taxes**. That's the complete price and a savings of 10% off the cover prices—what a great deal! I understand that accepting the 2 free books and gift places me under no obligation ever to buy any books. I can always return a shipment and cancel at any time. Even if I never buy another book from Harlequin, the 2 free books and gift are mine to keep forever.

186 HDN DZ72
386 HDN DZ73

Name	(PLEASE PRINT)	
Address	Apt.#	
City	State/Prov.	Zip/Postal Code

* Terms and prices subject to change without notice. Sales tax applicable in N.Y.
** Canadian residents will be charged applicable provincial taxes and GST.
   All orders subject to approval. Offer limited to one per household and not valid to
   current Harlequin Romance® subscribers.
   ® are registered trademarks owned and used by the trademark owner and or its licensee.

HROM04   ©2004 Harlequin Enterprises Limited

Like a phantom in the night comes
a new promotion from

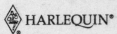 HARLEQUIN®

INTRIGUE®

GOTHIC ROMANCE

Beginning in August 2004, we offer you
a classic blend of chilling suspense and
electrifying romance, starting with....

A DANGEROUS INHERITANCE
LEONA KARR

And don't miss a spine-tingling Eclipse tale each month!

September 2004
MIDNIGHT ISLAND SANCTUARY
SUSAN PETERSON

October 2004
THE LEGACY OF CROFT CASTLE
JEAN BARRETT

November 2004
THE MAN FROM FALCON RIDGE
RITA HERRON

December 2004
EDEN'S SHADOW
JENNA RYAN

Available wherever Harlequin books are sold.
www.eHarlequin.com

HIECLIPSE